PENGUIN BOOKS
THE HOUSE THAT SPOKE

Zuni Chopra is a fifteen-year-old author who has published two books of poetry. She has a passion for fantasy writing and poetry, and her favourite authors include Neil Gaiman and Lewis Carroll. She lives in Mumbai with her parents, older brother and their six dogs. This is her first novel.

ADVANCE PRAISE FOR THE BOOK

'It beautifully captures the air, the fragrance, the culture, the relationships, the landscape of Kashmir . . . the true soul of Kashmir . . . a Kashmir that manages to retain its natural beauty, its culture and its essence of harmony in the midst of the black shadow of violence and bloodshed. More importantly, it captures the actual feelings of young Kashmiris, both Pandit and Muslim, who have, as in this book, experienced beauty . . . and peace in their homes, even though they are surrounded by violence and bloodshed'—Masood Hussain

'Extremely confident, lyrical and magical . . . I loved its Studio Ghibli qualities as in Miyazaki's *Spirited Away* or *Howl's Moving Castle*—but this is definitely a Zuni Chopra production. The backdrop is terrific and well handled'—Adrian Levy

'Merges fantasy and historical elements with the ills in modern Kashmir, coupled with a message of hope. Perhaps only a child could have the free-flowing imagination to conjure up a story like this. I was fascinated by the way it was told'—Amish Tripathi

The
HOUSE
That
SPOKE

Zuni Chopra

PENGUIN BOOKS

PENGUIN BOOKS

USA | Canada | UK | Ireland | Australia
New Zealand | India | South Africa | China

Penguin Books is part of the Penguin Random House group of companies
whose addresses can be found at global.penguinrandomhouse.com

Published by Penguin Random House India Pvt. Ltd
7th Floor, Infinity Tower C, DLF Cyber City,
Gurgaon 122 002, Haryana, India

First published in Penguin Books by Penguin Random House India 2017

Text copyright © Zuni Chopra 2017
Illustrations copyright © Devangana Dash 2017

All rights reserved

10 9 8 7 6 5 4 3 2 1

This is a work of fiction. Names, characters, places and incidents are either the
product of the author's imagination or are used fictitiously and any resemblance
to any actual person, living or dead, events or locales is entirely coincidental.

ISBN 9780143427841

Typeset in Adobe Garamond Pro by Manipal Digital Systems, Manipal
Printed at Thomson Press India Ltd, New Delhi

This book is sold subject to the condition that it shall not, by way of trade
or otherwise, be lent, resold, hired out, or otherwise circulated without the
publisher's prior consent in any form of binding or cover other than that in
which it is published and without a similar condition including this condition
being imposed on the subsequent purchaser.

www.penguin.co.in

*To my closest friends, Anjali, Ish and Shreya,
for all the times we escaped the world
to dream of something better*

And, as it has always been, to Kashmir

'You're not the same as you were before. You were much more . . . muchier. You've lost your muchness.'

Lewis Carroll

Chapter One

Kashmir, Bharat

1591

The Pandit stroked his tangled beard with the air of a man quite pleased with his work. He stood—one gnarled hand on his withered hip, his charcoal-coloured pheran billowing around his twined ankles, his turban heavy upon his wrinkled forehead—staring at the majestic infusion of wood and brick. A house. His house. His masterpiece. Life hummed through its wooden walls. Cloaked in chinar, enveloped by the snowy mountain range, it stared into the royal-blue evening sky. He could sense the magic flowing through it, and it made his success glow even brighter in the gentle moonlight. He leaned proudly against the sturdy, rough bark of the tree.

How pleased Emperor Akbar would be! Why, all the land would know of his glories . . . of his . . . but . . . no! No one must ever find this house! Perhaps it was better if . . . if no one were to know . . . it would not take away from the power of his house after all . . . it would only ensure its safety. He glanced up at the house once more.

It was indeed a masterpiece, of which only a single room was breathing.

1752

It was late—almost half past ten. A small troop of weary British soldiers was moving heavily through the thick dunes of darkened snow, their backs to the towering snow-capped mountain range, as they sought shelter in the maze of a frosted wood. Their gruff lieutenant, who was particularly exasperated with the icy, untameable winds of this treacherously exotic country, was barking directions at regular intervals between frustration and fatigue. But they'd lost their way so thoroughly in the cold winter's night that it was all they could do to keep walking. Their eyes stung and squinted against the sudden sharp gusts of air. White knuckles gripped at shiny, new, heavy metal weapons that had proved useless against the wilderness of the night. The trees above them were swathed in seas of freshly fallen snow, pressing against one another so that they cut off even the smallest glimmer of the scattered stars.

Kout I. Peterson, a small, unwieldy soldier of the troop, with a tuft of brown hair and a rather crooked nose, brought up the rear. Short as he was, he could barely see past the man in front of him. The muzzle of his thick, bloated weapon smacked against his reddening thigh as he pushed his protesting legs forward. His bad ankle was grinding against his bones, twisted and swollen, his socks thick and frigid with melted ice. Every now and then, he would feel his leg sink into a sinister, hidden pit of sleet, so that his rough, flat feet burnt from the cold. His tongue felt fat and heavy, his mouth parched.

There came a loud, jarring crack as his boot pressed down upon a crushed scrap of rusty metal oozing out like a bubble of blood on the pure silver landscape. Had it not been for this sudden noise, he would never even have realized the contact, for he could—thankfully—no longer feel his feet. He glanced down at his boot as though it were a stranger's, seeing it cutting into the dull glow of red iron jutting out from the shade of a fir tree. He thought abruptly and longingly of fresh cerise strawberry jam, dripping off warm, crusty white bread milled from the grains of the field, accompanied by steaming tea in his wife's new white china teacups. Ah, to be home! But home was some 5000 miles away. And with a sickening crunch he smacked painfully into reality—he was not home. He was here, in this uncivilized, bizarre and outlandish terrain, surrounded by blizzards and yetis and chilled, raw air, so far away from anything of value that he wondered if London had forgotten him.

What an honour it had been then, to write his name with great flourish upon the registration form, to receive his smart new uniform, to walk proudly into the pubs in the evenings and proclaim his undying patriotism, a patriotism he now felt was teetering on the brink of extinction. The futility and utter childishness of their task—to head to Rawalpindi and aid the army's trading company, which hoped to expand further west—seemed to weigh down upon him in the night.

Just then, as though some native angel had taken pity on his fate, he saw the smallest chinks of light begin to show themselves from behind the trees. The droplets of gold multiplied until they gently merged with one another and grew brighter, till finally, the troop burst out into a small clearing with an old, wooden house before them. For a moment, they were all struck by a feeling none of them could describe—a sudden calm, yet an undefined, strange sense of foreboding. Their eyes shifted to a towering, deep brown tree beside them, which looked like it had a river of paint flowing within, bringing out the colour each crevice held. Its branches stretched out above them, as though trying to catch the wind.

'Sir?' came the voice of one of the troop. 'Um . . . Lieutenant Hawthorne, sir? Are we spending the night here?' The lieutenant swung around at the question. He shook his head to throw off this lingering sense of curious apprehension at the welcoming warmth and shelter. He was the *lieutenant*, for God's sake! He had to pull himself together!

Shaking the snow off his weathered boots, he barked, 'Right then, gents, we've reached camp for the night. Tomorrow morning, up bright and early then, and we can ask this house for directions.' He paused a moment, biting his tongue and closing his eyes, before altering his sentence to fit his status. 'I meant, of course, the people in this house. Well, get yourselves in order then, and all change out of your pockets and handed over.'

There were a few grumblings from the soldiers.

'All change OUT of your pockets, I said!'

Once they'd handed over what he thought would be enough to persuade the owners to give them a room and some food, he climbed up the creaky front steps, taking care to avoid slicks of ice, and rapped sharply on the front door. For a few moments, there was no reply. The lieutenant was about to simply march in—that's just the sort of man he was, you understand—when the door was gently pulled open from the inside. In the doorway stood a young woman who seemed to be in her early thirties, callouses betraying her suffering, wide eyes her fear at facing strange men, pursed lips, her alien local speech.

Instantly, every man on the doorstep felt suffused with a cosy, quiet calm—not a heated, eerie sort of silence, but the calm that wafts like pure cotton around one's healing heart. They stood jovially in the doorway despite their chilled limbs, and the lieutenant spoke in a slow, loud voice that seemed to have lost its old gruff grunting about the weather and the soldiers and the time.

'Why, good evening, young lady. How do you do?' he began. 'My troop and I were looking for somewhere to spend the night. Would you be amic—kind enough to allow us a bedroom or two?'

She did not seem to understand, or perhaps she was simply formulating an acceptable reply. The lieutenant stood as patiently as his instinct allowed him, out on the porch under the dusty, white-flecked sky.

She opened her mouth tentatively, as though this was the first sentence she'd ever utter. But before she could respond, there came a great clattering of frantic footsteps. The lieutenant, who had been expecting to see a small horde of people, perhaps her children, raised his eyebrows as one scrawny, wrinkled man joined her at the door.

His face was a crumbling chaos of bumps and ridges, so that at first, his mouth had appeared to the troop as nothing more than another wrinkle chiselled into his leathery skin. His eyes burnt like sputtering torches within his frozen face. His twisted beard was short and scraggly, so scruffy that it resembled a bird's nest, abandoned for the winter. Strands of deadened, grey hair were squirming out of the thick, black turban resting over his shrunken head.

When he spoke, his voice came cracked and raspy through the cutting air. 'What you want with this place?'

'My troop and I would like to stay,' the lieutenant repeated. 'We're just passing through. We've lost our way, and we don't have anywhere else to go.'

The man's pupils grew wide and deep, a winter tempest reflected in the darkness of their depths. 'No!' he muttered angrily. 'No,' he repeated, louder then, his voice a thundering rumble. 'I sorry, but no one allowed to stay here.'

Lieutenant Hawthorne was on the verge—what with his own shivering shoulders and how comfortable the house seemed to be—of asking his men to shove their way in and make him tea, when he recalled they had another, universal means of persuasion at their disposal. He handed over the scraps of twisted banknotes clutched in his fat fist.

The woman inhaled sharply, her eyes darting from note to note, trying to quickly calculate how much it was. Her collarbone grew piercingly pronounced with the force of her shallow breath, her fingers suddenly fidgeting unceasingly, and her eyes betrayed her feverish excitement.

The man turned to her, his expression one of utmost indignation. 'No!' he repeated to her, looking astonished at her reaction. What he said next, they did not know, for it was said quickly and quietly, in a tongue they had neither heard nor heard of.

Her lip curled with something close to defiance as he spoke. She seemed to brush him off, her expression one of superior calm and control. Without waiting for any further retaliation, she snatched the wad from the lieutenant's clammy palm and bade them all come in.

They entered a small, cosy room, the sharp clicking of their boots cushioned by the carpet, whose soft wool swayed gently like bursting algae at the bottom of the shallowest sea. In the next room, they caught sight of a fireplace with some sort of carving on it. The blaze cackled merrily, lighting up the frosted crystals against the window's glass. The men made instantly for that room, presuming it to be the dining area. But before the lieutenant could follow his troop, their host gripped his hand with remarkable strength for the age of his rickety bones. He pointed towards a trapdoor, dusty and unused, lying towards the back of the room, and thrust his forearms together to make an X in front of the lieutenant's face. 'No,' he repeated with the air of a man trying his best to convince himself the world's problems could be solved if only people heeded simple instructions. 'You must no go there. Or you cannot stay. Right?'

'Right, sure,' the lieutenant replied. His host did not seem convinced, and stared at him reproachfully, the eyes boring through his skin.

Just to satisfy the old guy, Lieutenant Hawthorne snatched the closest troop member and, signalling pointedly at the trapdoor, bellowed, 'This is off limits, okay? Tell the rest of them.' The soldier nodded hurriedly, his skull rattling in his face, and then turned to pick up the plate he'd just dropped on the floor. The lieutenant turned back to his host only to find that he had yanked the carpet over the trapdoor and seated himself firmly upon it with a beady glint in his eye.

Then he waddled towards his dinner. Blasted foreigners.

Kout I. Peterson lay quiet and motionless in his sleeping bag, utterly and undoubtedly awake. He had turned himself over so many times that he'd quite forgotten which side he'd started on. The moth-eaten scrap of cloth their hostess had provided as a blanket barely covered his torso, and he was kept up by the consistent chattering of his own teeth. Moonlight gushed in through a nearby window, and was reflected brightly off the snowflakes outside. While it was breathtaking, it didn't lend itself to sleep.

Kout shut his eyes. He put a pillow over his head. He ran his hands over his small, round face. He counted sheep. He steadied his breathing. He tucked his knees up to his chin. He made up a story in his head. Getting a little desperate, he counted goats. Finally, he could simply no longer deny it. There was no way he was getting a wink of sleep tonight.

He looked enviously at his troop members, tangled about on the smooth wooden floor, half on and half off their sleeping bags, dreaming of the smell of home.

His stiff shoulders jerked with the cold. When he blinked, his eyes stung. Frustrated, he gave a great sigh and watched his breath steam up in the frosty air. That was the last straw.

Slipping out of his sleeping bag, keeping his blanket as warmly tucked around him as he could, he moved quietly towards the door, hoping to find some extra bed sheets or a heater. He scraped at the floor with the very tips of his toes, navigating his way through the jumble of sleeping bags that barred his way like fat bugs, trying not to wake the others. He was lucky; each plank of wood kept still and silent beneath his feet as he crept out of the room.

Standing in the doorway, he whisper-yelled to try and get his hostess's attention. But he didn't even know her name, let alone whether she understood his English. He moved slowly downstairs, wondering where she was sleeping and why she hadn't heard him. Just a deep sleeper, he assured himself.

But there was nothing in the darkened living room except a few small dust motes hovering in the silver air.

He backed out, his bad ankle catching on a latch beneath the carpet near the bottom of the stairs as he did so. He looked down with a jerk, surprised. Slowly, as though peeling away chipping wallpaper, he pulled the carpet off the ground, revealing a small brass latch hammered within the wood, deep crevices outlining a hidden door. Puzzlement formed furrows against his doughy skin. Could his hostess be there? Lowering himself to the ground, he cracked open the trapdoor, finding it was rather larger than he'd imagined, and looked inside.

Before he could raise it all the way, a series of small brass chains snapped to attention, preventing the opening from widening.

He was met with a low, prolonged hiss of steam from a tangled mass of rusty heaters. After letting out a slight 'Oh' of understanding, he felt his hopes rise fractionally for the first time that night. He didn't need to wake up his hosts, after all; he could simply turn up the heat and head back to bed.

A sting of irritation followed this realization. If only he could get past the chain locks. What was the need for his hosts to bolt up the boiler room? As though it carried a lost kingdom of wealth! They were just heaters, after all. Pulling out his penknife from his back pocket, he started to snap through the ageing metal cables. Despite the crack of rusty brass, no one seemed to hear him.

Finally, he pulled the trapdoor further up, the wood scratching against his nails, and caught sight of a small metallic flight of stairs leading down into the boiler room; he hadn't noticed it before.

But just as he made to hoist himself into a climbing position, an odd sensation quivered down his spine, like a snake slithering between his bones. He froze, his mouth dangling half-open and his eyes large and round. He turned his gaze once more to the heaters; they stared back up at him innocently—eerie, like possessed schoolchildren, quiet and calm.

Kout bit his tongue, sternly telling himself he'd imagined it. Yet he could not rip his unfocused gaze away. He shook his head, trying to clear it, and muttered to himself that he really ought to get back to bed. He made to reach for the trapdoor's handle—

And let out a wild gasp. He had felt it again—an odd, urgent sensation, as though something were closing in upon him. Something was down there . . . something dangerous. His first thought was to call his troop. Then he realized that if he pulled a stunt like that, they'd think he'd lost his marbles. And none of them would take kindly to being woken at a time like this for some vague imagining of his. He'd be in hot water with the lieutenant after less than a month of being in the army! No, he mustn't wake any of them up!

Slowly, tentatively, Kout placed his bare, rough heel on the first step. It pressed against him, a sliver of a tundra glacier rather than metal.

With each step, he knew with greater certainty that he ought to have turned back the step before, yet he couldn't turn away, lured by the call of a hidden siren.

When he reached the floor of the boiler room, nothing appeared out of the ordinary. He looked up at the carved wooden ceiling. Smudged flowers and birds sprawled out from an unassuming burst of blooms at the very centre. Just then, a sharp, painful tug in his gut made him turn to a depression in the ground. He knelt beside it, touched a finger to it, and was nearly overcome by a twisted, warped, miserable shadow of emotion, seeping from the indentation hacked into the stone floor.

He pushed away from it and took great gulps of air, leaning against a creaking boiler, trying to prevent his lungs from caving in. Then, slowly, as though consumed by the gentle fury of steam, he guided his fingers back to the edge of the emerging cusp, and pushed upwards so that an unseen, hulking pile of twisted rock and metal began, ever so slightly, to move. Hidden symbols, scriptures, he believed, glinted in the dim light. Detachedly he noted that he was beginning to feel distinctly hot around the collar. Then, with a final burst of effort, the roughly hewn hatch lurched to the sky, as though it had been dormant for centuries.

Black. All black. Then all at once, a figure ripped from the once hidden chamber, bursting forth from the sinking, suffocating pit—not emerging from the darkness, but darkness itself. A roar of triumph, majestic and horrifying, rang through the boiler room, so that it seemed to tear his skin from his warm flesh. For a moment, the smoke seemed to silhouette a figure in the night, disfigured and powerful, more terrible than he'd ever seen. Dry heat pulsated from the figure, and Kout was at a complete loss as to how he had ever been cold. He felt as though he had been thrown within the searing black flames of hell.

With a flick of a contorted limb, it dashed him to the ground. It was worse than any sea serpent, any dark nightmare, any mythical monster. He lay there, horrified, heart pounding as he stared into nothingness, terror, misery, death.

The smoke wafted to the ceiling. It disappeared. For a moment, Kout felt something akin to relief.

Then all he knew was festering flesh and rotting soul, foul terror and the blaze sapping the marrow from his scorching bones; skin and sinew smelting against what moments before had been a blood-red heart.

The Pandit normally took great care in ensuring he woke up just before dawn. He believed, naturally, that this was the time when the body's systems were refreshed and efficient, and hence a time when the mind could work extraordinary magic. He was accustomed to being easily woken by something as gentle as birdsong streaming through the window. So unsurprisingly, the shuddering explosion of crashes and heavy gusts of wind from downstairs had caused him to be thrown out of bed and on to the floor. He righted himself and rushed to the source of the noise, taking the stairs two at a time and panting for air, his rumpled beard sticking out at all ends and his turban unravelling as he went.

Upon arriving downstairs, he was met with a harrowing sight; every window had been smashed to jagged pieces, as though an insane beast had slashed through them. Slivers of darkness had crept in through the cracks and punctures in the house. Shattered glass lay against the wood, glinting in the slowly rising sun. Outside, through the open door, the Pandit saw that a stream of abruptly melted snow had created a haphazard, smoking path, as though a fireball had been launched from the house out into the valley. And the trapdoor to the hammam had been thrown wide open, hollow and empty as the Pandit's eyes.

Lieutenant Hawthorne hated mornings. It was too bright, too soon, and frankly, there was just too much left of the day. As such, mornings were his least favourite time to receive bad news. So it did put a bit of a damper on his otherwise pleasant disposition when he arrived downstairs to find that one of his troop members had died.

Their host, eyes wide and furious, limbs thrashing in every direction, seemed alternately to be yelling at his guests and his daughter, who dropped, sobbing and miserable, beside the open trapdoor. His cheeks were pink with fury, his teeth yellow and snapping against one another, and his nostrils flaring so wide that the lieutenant could almost see smoke pouring out of them, in addition to all the silvery nose hair poking out.

Leaving his men to sort things out for the moment, he surveyed the scene. The windows had been blasted open, the windowpanes dripping with melted ice. The door was hanging off a hinge, and outside, it seemed as though a sizzling horse had galloped through the snow, as though a hundred tongues of an inferno had carved a path into the ground, as though a hungry blaze had been flung into the valley. The forest they'd passed the night before had been burnt to a crisp, the woods black and thin like skeletons against the landscape. Snow had become water to reveal murky brown earth. The patch of sky above was engulfed in fog. Only the tree beside the house remained standing, serene and unruffled, as if watching the mildly entertaining proceedings. A fire had been started . . . or something had escaped . . . but what? Surely, it couldn't have been human . . . must be something . . . something satanic . . . but that was ridiculous, he muttered. He wasn't one to believe in spirits. And yet, despite his mind's reassurances, he felt fear beginning to creep up his spine.

His soldiers were looking down into the gaping opening, their faces contorted with disgust. As he neared them, he realized why; a horrible smell of burnt, festering flesh was rising from the chasm below.

Appalled, disgusted, some shaking with the shocking and unspeakable nature of their discovery, they saw Kout, his body charred and disfigured, flung face down near some sort of opening, and where that opening led, they were too far away to tell . . . some sort of deep cavern . . .

The woman, tears splattered across her thin, yellowing cheeks, threw herself in front, blocking their view, and spat at two of the soldiers to go recover the body. When they emerged, clutching it at the legs and shoulders, or whatever its extremities were, their compatriots let out loud gasps at the sight of the corpse. It seemed as though he had been scorched in open flame; his face could not be discerned from the rest of him. His flesh had sunk into the gaps of his bones, melted to charcoal. The occasional flash of filthy white displayed a cracking skull.

And yet the lieutenant was puzzled, his heart pounding as he turned his nose away from the stench, as there was not a sign of a blaze within that room. At least, he hadn't seen one. He gripped at the holster of the sword in his belt, terror making his body stiff and tense. Perhaps he could get a better look . . . convince himself that this had nothing to do with voodoo of any kind . . . he leaned forward . . .

The man slammed the trapdoor shut. Heat and energy radiated off him, his teeth gritted fiercely. Such was his unexpected strength and fury that the lieutenant was too startled to argue. Rather, his mind frantically burst into a series of incoherent thoughts, suggesting that perhaps his host was not wholly human either.

'Out!' he bellowed, his voice nearly cracking with the strain. 'You done this! All you! We were not to let you in here! Out! Out, and take that too!'

He pointed a grimy finger at what had once been Kout I. Peterson, age twenty-four, newest member of the troop, and was then an unrecognizable mess of scalded skin, blood and bone, grotesquely suspended like a Christmas decoration between two haggard members of the pultan.

'Let's go, men,' whispered the lieutenant, quiet with fright for the first time in his life, and utterly paralysed. The troop hurried out, shaking and pale, before he'd even choked out the words.

And before any of them could gather themselves together, or even deduce some sort of explanation for their comrade's murder, the front door slammed shut in their faces.

The jaundiced moon hung in the air like a disease, mirroring the sickness of the earth. Darkness seeped through the black waters of Dal Lake, rotting the lotus blooms at its surface, shikaras utterly still, as though afraid to reveal themselves to the night. Hungrily, Kruhen Chay swept through the immobile trees. Once again, he felt warped elation at his power. So easy it had been to spot the weakest. To freeze him where he slept. To force the soldier into breaking the bars of his cage. All those years, trapped, worse than a mere shadow. Then, free at last.

He spied a farmer, back bent with labour and age, scrabbling at the dense, infertile soil with a thick, rusty shovel. Kruhen Chay felt a cruel thrill go through him at the sight of such helpless pain. He could sense the farmer's weary, collapsing house just a few feet away. Inside it, his wife and their young daughter, beauty taken by labour, scraped the rot off their dinner. His old mother was sitting quietly in the corner and trying not to die in her sleep.

With a snarl, Kruhen Chay lunged at the farmer, engulfing him, and as he pulled away, he heard the short cry as the farmer clutched at *his broken back and sank to his knees, burns and blisters erupting across his skin, life rapidly leaving his shrivelling lungs. With the cold satisfaction of victory, the darkness felt his body become longer, stronger, denser. Mist became hard muscle and sinew from the chill of a farmer's grief. A distorted human limb, the first of many, began to grow from his side. Inside the house, someone screamed.*

Chapter Two

Present Day

*S*omewhere in northern India, so far away that you can't hope to see it unless you perhaps crane your neck, there's a line on the ground. It's a nasty little line, because no one ever seems to agree on it. It moves this way and that, being thrust about fiercely, but it never seems to stop. Map after map is printed and fixed, adjusted by a centimetre—the Line of Control must, of course, be drawn exactly right. And they rage at each other over and over again, over this little line, murdering at random as an expression of how much they care.

You can just see it if you look carefully, and push up on your toes a bit. It's right here.

What's that? Can't see anything?

Well, of course not! There's nothing there really . . . it's just a mark they've made up in their heads . . .

I live in a fairy tale. Or rather, I live in the house of a fairy tale. The great Mughals themselves could not have crafted a palace to compare with my haven of wonders, nestled away in the valley of Kashmir.

The house is surrounded by shrubs and trees, and is almost humble in its shy seclusion. A jade-green and lavender vine exults in thin, blushing blossoms that emerge in spring and retreat once more in autumn; the vine grows up around the window, as though fondling it to brush away its tears at the many cracks sprinkled upon it.

Beside this window, a tall, magnificent chinar stands rooted and firm against the house. Its leaves are light green, lush and verdant in spring, and then grow deeper and deeper until, by summer, their colours become vivid and rich as darkened seaweed. But it is in autumn when I like its leaves best—when they shine a glinting gold like the last flaming stars in a blackening sky. This chinar has been there for as long as I can remember; it is a friend to me.

A chimney erupts almost gracefully from the tattered roof, and often smoke flies out of it, rushing to freedom. The roof itself is battered from the many beatings of rain and snow.

A layer of uncut grass spreads itself out into surrounding areas, and the weeds frolic in the small garden of olive green. The garden extends past our thin fence, into the trees of pine and chinar, all the way up to those mountains over there. Often, I wonder if I will climb them some day.

The house is made entirely of redwood, except for the chimney, which is brick. The door waits upon the frail doorstep, cordial and respectful. The house is poised, modest, meek and bashful, almost afraid of the brash and brazen houses that swagger beyond the many trees that surround it. The tranquil atmosphere envelops the house, wafting through the door and settling with a sigh upon the furniture.

The furniture, quiet and mellow, is made of the finest chinar wood and highly polished. It is cleanly cut and timeless, giving a mythical feel to the house. My great-grandfather carved much of it himself, they tell me.

The immaculate carpet, faded yet soft and warm, sleeps upon the well-worn floor and muffles your footsteps as if to say that silence is golden, which is why not a sound echoes through the house. The walls are smooth and warm, and keep me inside their cosy folds, comforting when the rest of the world seems black.

The windows invite the rays of light to burst through them. They are, however, not as large as they believe; you can see but the occasional dapple of light upon the floor, shining through from the garden outside.

The windows are only at the front of the house, though. At the back, there are none, for Ma likes to say that one should always look to the future and not be stuck in the past. Sometimes I feel she says it more to herself than to me.

A single desk and chair stare curiously out of a window, as aged as the rest of the furniture. Resting upon the desk is a long, feathery white quill dipped in navy ink, a prized family heirloom. The front room also holds a small cooking stove and a few mismatched cupboards stuffed with pans. I'm always careful to open them slowly, lest a pot tumble out at first chance. When the stove is lit, it immerses the room in the sharp scent of spice, the salty smell of melting butter, the sizzle of cooking meat.

On the second floor, there are two small rooms. One of them is a library, or, at least, I call it one—it's what one calls a place filled with books. In the corner of the room is a puffy armchair with worn-out pillows that grow softer as the years go by. I bury my face in its velvety surface and bounce upon the fluffy chair, or, for the mellow Sundays, curl up with a good story and a fresh cup of kehva. Broad bookshelves lean against the walls, bursting with hundreds of dusty books. Magic awaits in their worn, yellowed pages.

Next to the library is a bedroom with a small, cushiony bed, an embroidered bed sheet dotted with faded chinar leaves thrown upon it. The right side is mine, and the left, Ma's. Portraits of maharajas, ranis, Sufi saints, brave rajkumars and mystical creatures from old folk tales add colour to the walls. The back wall is crowded with pictures of the ancient Pandits, my ancestors. The oldest one on the far left is a charcoal painting, and over the years I've surmised that it was a self-portrait. Slowly, they segue into watercolour, and then a mixture of pencil and paint. Only the four at the very end are in print. They've been in my family for ages. Tathi says she doesn't want them sold.

The arid room with an uncluttered bed is a sanctuary for dreams. They drift lazily around the tender bed, filling my head as I lie down to sleep at night. They nestle in every corner of the room, but mainly in the pillows. The blanket is light and gentle—a shield from the crisp air of the room.

The room at the very back of the house on the lower floor has a small fireplace, lightly embossed with a family crest, so worn at the edges that I often run my fingers across it to make sure it's still there. But it never chips, cracks or darkens. Ma simply shrugged when I asked her how. It must be another perk of living here. Tathi has told me it is made of the finest stone, firm and strong. It has to be, to have lasted something like 400 years.

The crest bears two swans, which I've always imagined to be a soft, delicate pink, like an almond tree in bloom. They are embracing a third swan in their wings. I think it shows how much the family cares for each other. Ma says it shows our ancient roots and how our lineage in Kashmir goes back generations.

Underneath the crest is a pile of sullen logs, sprinkled with soot and ashes. They simply lie, broken and defeated, in the hearth. When the fire is made, mainly during winter, when the world outside is a sparkling white, the flames lick the roof of the roaring fireplace. I see magic leaping inside the haven of the fire. Ancient stories written long ago—of heroes, monsters and warriors—come alive in the frosty winter inside the gleaming fire, inside the jewelled fireplace. They are ablaze with a life inside them that I always hope to have. The fiery heat warms me from the inside and I shut my eyes, completely focused on the fire in front of me. The tantalizing scent of flame fills the room and keeps us in a silent agreement that life is beautiful and we are content.

Come spring, the cherry trees are in full bloom. Their fragile blossoms are silvery and white. Ruby-red roses dot the bushes, and butterflies flutter in and out of the vines that grow around the house. The nargis send their heavenly fragrance to mesmerize onlookers; the peppery smell of

Ma's tomato plants are in sharp contrast. Crunchy crimson and light green apples burst through the scintillating scents of the garden. The leaves of the plants surrounding us are a vivid evergreen. They shine like newly minted silver when the clouds sprinkle water upon their criss-crossing network of roots. The hibiscus flowers are a pearl white and a blush pink, with an exquisite aroma that causes me to become light-headed. The pine trees that lie dotted over the landscape reach upward to touch the sky and rain needles upon the grassy floor.

This is my home. It speaks to me. This is the house that takes me in when I've had enough of the world. This house is a pearl that resides in the oyster of my heart. Though all must some day waste away, and the world will some day end, this house will live on till the days vanish into ash, and time and death, brothers in arms, engulf the rest of the world.

My mother never leaves a thread undone. I see it in her hair, the way it coils impeccably around itself, no more than a few strands astray. I see it in the way she walks, at ease yet upright, fixing things that bend at odd angles or shutting windows left so slightly ajar you could almost miss their breeze. I see it most of all in her threads themselves, in the way they entwine with each other like gnarled, twisted stumps of decaying oak; in the way they wind themselves lovingly around her fingers, and slip into position just as she draws them away.

But sometimes, my mind wanders to forbidden lands, and it whispers that perhaps . . . perhaps the reason she meticulously brushes each light brown strand into place every morning is because there are far too many loose, chaotic, forgotten ends in her life to possibly tie up again.

The fresh autumn morning was just beginning to bloom. It seemed as though the sky had slept in, and slept well, and was thoroughly happy about it. I always make it a point to awaken to the sight of the mountains—their crevices creating rivers of gushing snow, small trees dotted across the lush green landscape at their feet, sun blazing above their shining white peaks. I kept the curtain closed halfway, however, since Ma was sleeping and she'd been up late the night before, cleaning. I opened the window slightly and took in a great gust of cool air. The wind seemed to dance across my sleepy eyes. Outside, the chinar swayed lazily in the breeze, the rays of sunlight gleaming on its leaves.

Pulling away, I closed the window as gently as I could. The paintings were quite silent. The Mughal warrior leaned back in his frame, his dark hair covered by a shiny metal helmet, his face relaxed and young, his moustache long and excessively curly, and his frame tilted at the angle he liked. His long, regal robe of deep blue was bunched up in a corner of the frame. Despite all that was said about the prestige it added to his figure, his outfit still looked like a dress to me.

Suddenly, with a jolt, I remembered—my dress! I hurried over to the closet, forgetting, in my excitement, to be quiet. Not that it mattered; our carpet, glowing red and black in the morning sunlight, always muffles any noise. You may be old or young, good or evil, angrez or local; it doesn't matter. For the brief space of time in which your skin touches her cloth, you are her child, in all the ways that matter.

I really hoped I'd remembered to put my dress back in the closet! I flung open the door and—yes, there it was! It's one of my favourite dresses because of its deep lilac hue. I don't own anything else that's purple. It had accidentally got caught in the front door the day before, and had a wide tear. I took it out of the closet, just to have a look, and ran my hands smilingly over the soft, mended cloth.

My stomach growled, and I realized I was famished. Though it was breakfast time, I longed suddenly for Tathi's rogan josh. My mouth watered at the thought of the spices, the crisp-on-the-outside, soft-on-the-inside mutton, the occasional red chilli immersed in the crimson curry and the taste of it all mixed with soft, light Kashmiri rice.

I told myself sternly to stop that kind of thinking. It wasn't doing my poor stomach any favours. Before hurrying down, I paused to glance in the mirror. My fingers tugged at the end of my loose, discoloured T-shirt. My two front teeth still stick out a bit, but I can't help that. The dimple on my left cheek, once my testament to lasting beauty, had faded when I was nine. My jet-black hair fell across my shoulders in tangled waves. I was somewhat untidy, since I'd been asleep so long, but not altogether unpresentable. I caught my eye in the mirror. Wait—hold on—well, surely my hair looked better than *that*!

The mirror rippled over, appearing liquid glass, then reformed again. My fringe lay nicely across my forehead, no longer as bushy and scattered as it had seemed a moment earlier. With a small nod of approval at myself, I turned to leave the room.

I took the steps two at a time, hoping I could see Tathi sometime soon. Ma always said I had her brown eyes. I missed her food, of course, but most of all, I missed her stories. She'd told me such fantastic ones lately! My favourite was the story of Jalodbhava, the water demon that had once inhabited the lake our homeland had been ages ago, once immortal in its murky depths; but as Lord Vishnu drained his lake, he fled through the valley, only to be met with our patron deity, who brought about his end by crushing him with a boulder. It was a bit ironic, given that Tathi couldn't read. I liked to sit by Tathi's fire as she recounted these fantastical tales to me, and then fall asleep by her knee. The carpet was just perfect for such things.

It was a pity she found it difficult to come over to our house; Gupkar Road had been her home, too, when she was younger, but she hardly visited any more. Ma said it was just her age. Whenever the story reached its end, she'd do up her squat, white bun again. She held it up with two black chopsticks. She wore thick, round glasses that were terribly old, but she said they held too many memories for her to change them.

It was a long walk to her place, but I made up my mind to visit her as soon as I could. Maybe even in time for lunch!

I reached the living room. Morning sunlight poured in from the window. I could just make out dewdrops on the grass. It must have been chilly outside.

I was just wondering what I'd have to eat when I heard Ma coming down the stairs. I went to hug her good morning, throwing my arms around her chubby centre, and she smiled a rather tired smile, patting me on the back. Her chestnut-coloured hair was already twisted back into a bun, some strands still sticking out with morning frizz. Her eyes, however, were shining from a good rest.

'I wish you'd wait a moment before putting your hair up. It looks so lovely when it's loose!'

'Zoon, I don't like it falling over my shoulders like that. Now, are you hungry?'

Changing the subject again. Well done, Ma.

Well, I *was* hungry.

In a few moments, Ma had provided me with a fresh, steaming hot chapatti. We had leftover haak from last night, so I was promptly served some of that as well.

'I know, I know,' she said as I stared rather morosely at my plate, 'it isn't the finest of breakfasts. Well, I'll go out to get some fresh food as soon as I'm ready; I'll bring back something you like.'

I wolfed down my meal, secretly quite satisfied but not wanting to pass up the chance to have mithai after dinner. 'Jalebis!' I said, my mouth full to bursting. 'Ooh, and laddus, you must get some of those . . . what else . . .'

'Remember,' Ma said, cutting into my reverie before walking up the steps, 'Chandani, Lameeya and Rani Auntie are coming over for lunch, so you'd better clean yourself up a bit and be polite once they're over, all right?'

I groaned. I couldn't even visit Tathi! 'Ma! Why must *I* be here when they're over? It's incredibly boring, and Chandani Auntie hugs like an elephant!'

Ma tried to look disapproving, but the corners of her mouth twitched slightly. 'Never mind that, you just make sure you're ready.'

I tugged disdainfully at my horrible, deep red salwar kameez, somehow wanting Tathi's cooking more than ever despite my tummy feeling unreasonably full. It didn't show, thank goodness; this was Ma's dress, and so it was a bit loose for me.

'I bet I look like I'm wearing a garbage bag,' I griped at Ma as she came down into the living room.

'Hush, and get yourself off the carpet.'

I scowled. Until a moment before, I had been lying sprawled on the soft, welcoming carpet, in front of the door.

I pulled myself up, flopped down on the wooden chair, put my head on the desk and pretended to be asleep while Ma came over to try and jam plastic red bangles down my wrist.

Just as they made it past my palm, the doorbell rang. Ma paid me and my bangles no more attention than if we had been a part of the wallpaper.

The door was promptly flung open, and a horde of gossiping ladies were welcomed in.

'Oh, Shanti, how *delightful* to see you!'

'I smell jalebis! Still the same sweet tooth, I see!'

'Goodness, the house looks wonderful! Your garden's really coming along! And—is that . . . Zoon? Why, you'd never recognize her! How she's grown!'

I braced myself for the inevitable. Determined to get Chandani Auntie out of the way first, I walked towards the trio.

Unfortunately, Rani Auntie, decked in some sort of itchy sari and her signature bright yellow shawl, was the first to pull me into her grasp. She was a short, hearty woman, with pink on her cheeks no matter what the season, and a bit of a weakness for sweets, just like Ma. In fact, that's how they met; they were both haggling over gulab jamun, and, having secured a satisfactory bargain for each other, became friends.

Rani Auntie pulled me into a big hug, patting me roughly on the back, saying, 'My, my, what a young lady she's become!'

Next up was Chandani Auntie, who seemed to want to make up for not being the first to hug me by ensuring that half of my bones were utterly broken and the other half nursing hairline fractures. She was a large, loud woman, our closest neighbour, who seemed to think that everything required her unnecessarily copious attention—especially me. For a good minute, she praised my bangles, my hair, my manners, my maturity, until finally, Lameeya Auntie came to—well, I can't say my rescue—push me straight out of the frying pan into the fire, shall we say.

She was a thin, bony woman, yet her smile was warm and caring. She stood straight-backed, as though one slip and she'd be left a hunchback for the rest of her life. Her teeth were a bit too white, her eyes a deep, swirling black. She lived just down the street and she and Ma had gradually grown fond of each other. Her husband, Bhasharat Uncle, was the much respected *ghodewala* of the town; he was also highly entertaining and very lively.

Today she wore a flowing pheran with zari embroidery blooming around her long neck and wrists. She patted me delightedly on the head and then said, 'I'm sure you and Altaf are going to be great friends! He's been away at boarding school, so he doesn't know a lot of people here.'

I hadn't the slightest idea what she meant until she moved aside, revealing a tall, gangly boy, his hair a deep brown and flopping in layers, hiding most of his forehead. His cheeks were pink with the chill and chubby like a child's. Altaf offered an awkward smile that spoke plainly of how little say he'd had about being there. As for me, I thought he looked a bit like a horse.

I let out an 'Oh!' of recognition. An old memory, inexplicably fished out of some hidden corner of my brain, surfaced before me like a faded Polaroid, blurred at the edges by its age—watching curiously as a young boy played catch on his own in the garden so near ours, laughing every time he fell over, and sitting sulky and sullen on the front steps when his brother snatched the ball away. I'd spoken to him once too. I'd just been asking about the time, so not a very meaningful conversation necessarily, but I remembered thinking he was quite decent to have run back inside to check for me.

The trio had moved as one, like a herd of buffaloes, to the back room. I hadn't even noticed that Ma had spread some pillows about. Once they'd planted themselves on the carpet, she made to get some kehva. She smiled at Altaf before whispering to me, 'What are you standing there like a goldfish for, Zoons?'

Startled, I went about moving my frozen limbs. Turning around, I nodded at Altaf, feeling that he warranted some sort of acknowledgement, before dragging my feet a few steps and dropping down on to the bottom stair, already tired of a conversation that hadn't even begun.

'So, Shanti, do tell! How's your boutique going? I bought the most beautiful shawl yesterday, but you weren't at the shop,' began Rani Auntie.

Ugh.

'Oh, all well, all well! Raj is as nice as ever, he always lets me take the unfinished ones home. Can't be at work all the time, you know. I don't like leaving Zoon home alone for too long.'

Why not? I'm not a baby! And besides, it's not like I'm ever craving for company! I thought.

Altaf joined me on the bottom step. I stared at him. He stared at his toes. I gave it up.

'Oh, of course! Do you know, *I've* been left home alone this morning!'

She gave a tinkling laugh.

'Yes, Bhasharat has gone with our eldest, Majid, to the mosque for morning prayer! I made them a few wish knots. Just to make sure they spend their time wisely!' said Lameeya Auntie.

The others joined in, giggling. I'd never been to the mosque.

Altaf huffed indignantly; clearly he hadn't been deemed old enough to join them. I didn't, of course, say it, but it seemed quite clear to me why; despite the fact that he was much taller than me, I'd never have guessed him to be my age. His gaze shifted around the room, glazed over with mild interest yet not taking anything in. And it was then that I noticed a pencil stuck behind his left ear, almost as though he'd forgotten it there.

'Oh, how lovely! I used to go to the temple every day, too, you know. They grow up so fast! Just look at Zoon! You must have your hands full, Shanti,' Chandani Auntie chirped.

'Oh, it's easy when they're as well behaved as she is. You're quite right, though; time really does flash by. Incredibly, in little more than a week, she'll be fifteen! But in some ways, it was easier when she was younger. I remember when I told her it was bad luck to stay up past one's bedtime!'

'What?' I whispered outrageously to myself amidst more chiming laughter. I still believed that!

I heard a stifled laugh and turned irritably to see Altaf staring innocently out of the window.

'Yes, fifteen is going to be a bit of a challenge, Shanti! But now that she's older, you can leave the house more often, come to the temple with me for Navaratri, perhaps,' Chandani Auntie suggested eagerly.

'Well . . . if there's time . . . I keep a fast anyway.'

'Goodness, I've only just remembered! Have you heard? Kheer Bhawani has changed colour again!' burst out Rani Auntie. Clearly she'd been waiting for an opportune moment in the conversation to reveal this.

They all gasped loudly, greatly excited.

What did that mean? I turned to Altaf. Seeing my raised eyebrows, he whispered, 'It's the famous pond, you know, that changes colour according to the current fate of Kashmir. Ma really puts a lot of stock in such things . . . sometimes I think a tad too much . . .'

I smiled. Leaning towards the desk and chair, I muttered, 'Sounds just like her, doesn't it? Sometimes I think she must be a bit—'

'Are you talking to yourself?'

I looked back to see Altaf frowning at me, confused. Turning sunset red, I stammered, 'No, no . . . um . . . I was just . . .'

Chandani Auntie's bellow carried clearly from the back room, rescuing me from having to respond. 'What colour is it now, Rani?'

'Well . . .' She sounded uncomfortable, as though she didn't feel like answering, as though responding with any conviction would make the occurrence an inescapable truth that would dampen the merry chatter.

'Black.'

There was an impenetrable pause.

'But you know, that was two days ago . . .' she added hurriedly.

'Why, of course. I'm sure it won't be long before it reverts again, if it hasn't already . . .'

That pause again.

'Well . . . I mean . . . it *has* got a bit worse lately, hasn't it?'

I was amazed at how hoarse Rani Auntie's voice had become.

'Without a doubt!' squawked Lameeya Auntie, and I heard her sniffing angrily, as she always did when her temper ran high but her dignity ran higher. 'It's insufferable! Military posts every mile you walk, barbed wire running through the fields, everyone always on the alert! I mean, sometimes I really wonder whether this is the best place for a family raising two young children . . .'

Altaf made a small noise in his throat. It sounded as though he meant it to be contemptuous but chickened out at the last minute. He hardly looked surprised, though; unlike me, he had heard this before, and gave me a tired grin. 'This discussion's been done to death, don't you think?' he put in, an attempt at light-heartedness.

I bit the inside of my cheek. 'It's like we start out free and fast-paced, and keep hitting the same dead end every time,' I replied. 'And we've no clue where to go from there, obviously, so we just keep going in circles, hoping to find something new.'

He blinked at me for a second, and then nodded slowly. 'Right. Yeah. I was thinking the same. Um . . . you're almost fifteen, right?'

'Yeah.'

He puffed out his chest, filling up with air, tossing back the hair that flopped against his eyes. '*I'm* fifteen and a half already,' he said, his glances at me betraying a certainty that this would earn him the utmost respect.

I nearly laughed, but passed it off for an impressed gasp at the last second.

'I mean, my brother's always been older, of course, but I'm catching up to him!' he finished proudly.

'How enthralling!' I replied. Concealing my grin in the loose sleeve of my kameez, I feigned attention as Chandani Auntie's heated voice came from the living room once more.

'No, it's impossible,' Chandani Auntie agreed. 'Do you know my business has dropped considerably?' she added after a beat.

Ma finally spoke.

'But . . . why . . .?'

'NO TOURISTS!' Chandani Auntie barked, probably rising half out of her chair.

Altaf jumped in the middle of scratching his nose, poking himself in the eye and cursing under his breath.

'And how exactly am I supposed to sell a single carving if there's NO ONE to SELL IT TO?'

'Horrible, horrible . . .' murmured Ma. 'Yes, I've noticed the drop in customers too . . .'

Had she? She never told me about it!

'Well, I don't blame them. Who'd want to be woken up with gunfire every morning?' put in Lameeya Auntie.

'Okay, that's exaggerating . . .'

'But, Rani, you must admit, it's getting worse and worse every week! Bombs being thrown about, my neighbour's son gone blind in the firing, such violence in the streets almost daily! And with riots every second sunrise, why, I shouldn't think it was safe to come near here at all!'

Rani Auntie fell silent.

At last, as everyone was shepherded out of the door, with cries of keeping well and meeting again soon, and Altaf having his hair ruffled five times over, I waved goodbye before sinking tiredly against the wall.

It is a curious thing, but I have noticed that doing nothing at all often expends more energy than leaping about on one's feet all day.

I glanced out of the window. The sky was bordering on a delicate pink, clouds wafting a subtle orange, gentle stars beginning to wake, the sun about to sink gracefully against the mountains, behind the chinar tree. The houses outside, our neighbours, some with thatched roofs, some with metal slats, only a few with bricks, seemed to stand firm without a sweltering sun melting them down. I could see the trio breaking up further down the road, in the shade of the lush, tall willow trees, waving and laughing before turning their separate corners and heading off.

It was evening.

Far away, perhaps somewhere nearer the centre of town, a gunshot sounded. Snarls, shouts and yelps came tearing after it, bursting through the streets, some drunk with anger, others with power, all swaying dangerously, destructive and unstable. This was followed by a series of angry hollers, whether for intimidation or encouragement, I could not tell.

Vaguely hoping to go up to the library to find a good book, I turned away from the window.

'Zoons! Come to the living room.'

'Ma, now?'

'I'll only be a moment.'

I walked towards the living room to find Ma stoking the fire. Its embers shimmered and crumbled around each other, burning from the inside out, beginning a small, steadfast flame. She stared pensively into its depths, as though expecting to see something more than red and gold. When she straightened up, I saw two dry red mirchis clutched tightly in her right hand and very nearly rolled my eyes.

'Ma!' I complained. 'Seriously? There's no *buri nazar* near *here*.'

'Well, everyone was admiring you in your lovely salwar kameez, and it's better to be safe than sorry, isn't it?'

With the precision of a magician, she rotated the mixture of chillies, rock salt and dry mustard seeds, thrice clockwise and thrice anticlockwise, spinning me around once or twice as she did so. Finally, she pressed them to my forehead and uttered a murmured prayer. Then she thrust the mixture into the fire. It crackled loudly, furiously—a demon unleashed, which was destroyed by the flame. We waited, but no fumes were released, no telling smoke that betrayed innocence, and slowly, the chillies turned black. 'There,' Ma said triumphantly. 'I told you so! You mustn't leave things like that in the air.'

I gave a small huff, defeated.

'Altaf asked if you could come over sometime. To play cricket.' She smiled, foreseeing my response.

I pretended to think hard. 'The former, maybe. The latter . . . hmm . . . let's say, never in a million years.'

She chuckled, seating herself by the fire. Her finger began swirling at the heated marble where it melded with the carpet, eyes intent on some point at the centre of the blaze, waiting for it to shine with hidden starlight, revealing a deep night sky within an inferno of light.

Somehow, she seemed abruptly blown away by myriad trains of thought, which had all left the station at once and had had a terrible collision on the tracks. Suddenly, she appeared as a king lost for orders, a mask lost for a human face, a writer lost for words.

I watched her for a moment, a bit puzzled by this unprecedented contemplation, and then turned to go upstairs.

It was a bright night. Too bright. He looked up at the full moon and snarled, deep and shuddering, creating abysmal furrows in the dry earth beneath him. He moved closer. The house radiated warmth, as did that pathetic shrub before it. But yet . . . it had softened. It was weakening every day.

With a gentle hiss that promised death, Kruhen Chay lunged at the chipped, tumbling chimney—and was thrown back with a resounding force, so that he felt a part of him revert once more to empty shadow, harmless as the twinkling stars. He cried out in agony—a guttural, animalistic wail, smarting with maddening frustration. Their Guardian—whoever he was—would not yield. It was this Guardian, he knew, this concentration of gushing magic, this embodiment of all things that opposed him, which was shielding the house, preventing his entry still.

And it was then that he was struck with an idea, his lips melting into a smile, the air around him growing thick and foul.

Yes. A Guardian—his Guardian. His weapon to use at his will. A vessel to pour himself into, an

accumulation of darkness rather than light. To strike just when their defences seemed weakest. Twisted elation rose up in him at the idea of victory—finally, victory—after all these years of pathetic, agonizingly fruitless struggles.

But—no! He would never need humans again! He had seen to that! He could not, would not ask a human for aid; it was too much to ask of his pride . . .

Ruefully, hatefully, bitterly, he forced himself to accept it.

He'd find himself a useful human, he promised, to bind himself to. A human who was easy to bend to his will, a human who had already allowed him to worm his way into their pathetic, empty heart. A human who, thus, would never fight his dominance, would never doubt his control, would never question his power.

A human who had enough influence of his own to give him what he needed.

A house.

That house.

Devoured.

Chapter Three

A few days had passed since Ma's friends had been over. What promised to be the last splatters of autumn rain were beating against the slopes of the valley. Occasional raindrops pelted against the window, trickling down the glass. The world outside was clear water and jade-blue evening, and they melded and fused till one was the other, and not even the creator could have told where they joined.

Just as I turned from the window and moved to go downstairs, a moment of lethargy gripped me by the shoulders and I slumped back on to the bed. I landed face first, like a sack of flour, my cheek pressed against the soft, white, embroidered cotton. My eyes fell on Ma's poetry book, kept carefully on the bedside table, the book she loved to read from every night. My head began to swirl with her favourite lines, lines she read out to me on nights we stayed up together, and I smiled. My eyelids fluttered closed.

A sharp rapping at the front door wrenched them open again. Irritated and indignant, I picked myself up from the bed. Why, I'd never known anyone to knock as impatiently as that! I stuck my head out of the doorway.

Just then, Ma zipped down the stairs like a cannonball. She shot past me, as indifferent to me as if I'd been part of the door, not even noticing when the end of her salwar caught and tore on the banister. After a moment of surprise, I followed her. Who on earth was this guest that she was so eager to greet? Surely, then, it couldn't be someone I'd seen before!

Straightening her dupatta hurriedly to cover up the rip—which, I noticed, was one of those special ones she didn't use often—Ma flung the door open.

In the doorway stood the most repellent little man with a pineapple of a nose. His hair was utterly black and slicked across his scalp. His long, thin face threw his bulbous nose into further relief.

'Zoon,' began Ma, after pleasantries had been exchanged, a little out of breath from the speed with which she had run to the door, 'I'd like you to meet Mr Qureishi.'

'Is this your daughter, Mrs Razdan?' he inquired politely before leaning across the threshold to shake hands with me.

Cautiously, I placed my hand in his large, rough palm for one quick shake. I was utterly unable to take my eyes off that nose. Monstrous!

'Yes, this is Zoon,' Ma said with a most un-motherly giggle. 'Oh, where are my manners? Do come in!'

She stepped away from the doorway to allow him inside. I gritted my teeth slightly as he crossed the threshold.

He wore a crisp black suit with a smart, stiff black tie, entirely devoid of crinkles. His shoes were polished so thoroughly I could see my own apprehensive face reflected in them. He carried a small nut-brown briefcase with the words

'Mihir R. Qureshi' stamped across them in faded gold. In other words, he did not look the type who had come for a gossipy luncheon.

So why was he here?

He shook his drenched umbrella outside, and then left it leaning against the wall next to ours. The door closed gently, shutting out the noise of the rain all at once, as though cutting short the fierce roaring of a mythical dragon in the night.

'Chai? Kehva? Coffee?' Ma offered, ignoring the fact that we didn't have any coffee.

'Oh, no, thank you. I'd have loved to stay for some kehva, but I must hurry. I've another appointment after this, and it will take me an unbearable amount of time in this downpour.'

I looked at him disgustedly. What was he blaming the rain for? Did he expect the universe to bend itself to his appointments?

'We'll hurry along then.'

Ma gestured around vaguely. 'We call this the front room,' she spluttered. 'We've a small cooking range over there . . . and . . . some windows . . .'

He raised his eyebrows at the quill resting against the wall in a small, dark blue inkpot seated on the beautifully carved desk. He extended one long finger and touched the length of the smooth wooden surface, as though checking for dust. I fought the urge to smack his hand away.

'Ma,' I said slowly, 'can you tell me what this is about?'

'Hmm?' she replied, looking purposefully vague. 'Oh, and that's the living room! We've a fireplace in there . . . not much . . . very old . . . I was thinking of adding a few chairs and things . . .'

Was she? Why? We loved sitting on the floor, she knew that!

Mr Qureishi followed Ma into the living room, his gaze lingering on the family crest. 'That's been there for as long as I've lived here. I've never thought of having it removed,' Ma said, tracing his gaze.

'Oh, no need to. It's charming.' His eyes shimmered for a moment. Yet he sounded as though he found it as dull as a maths textbook.

'Thank you . . . It's always been a . . . a rather unusual house . . . Upstairs?' Ma offered.

His gaze clung to the fireplace. 'Do you know, many people would be quite interested in having the family crest of a Pandit on their fireplace. Indeed a potential selling point.'

What? What on earth was he talking about? I gritted my teeth.

The upstairs bedrooms had been even worse. He told Ma that he liked what she'd done with the library, though he stared at the dusty bookshelves as though the books were not at all to his taste. He planted himself on the squashy armchair and pronounced himself satisfied with the 'aura' of the room. And then he had the audacity to step into the bedroom and smile—or whatever it was he did with his mouth (it had been quite overshadowed by his nose)—at the paintings of Mughal warriors, saints and rulers, particularly those of the Kashmiri

Pandits at the head of the bed. Finally, with the corners of his mouth tilted ever so slightly upwards, he turned to speak to my mother.

'I am pleased with the interior of the house, Mrs Razdan. You've retained a great deal of the house's history, which always attracts many buyers. We've already got a few potentials lined up, you know. If we added heating, and perhaps a television or a stereo on that desk with the feather, we'd have the deal closed in no time. I'm so happy you've decided to sell.'

An insidious fury had been rising up within me and it burst out, as though from an overfilled balloon, sudden and intense. 'Sell?' I didn't bother keeping my voice down. It thudded against the walls and seemed to be a solid object expanding between me and the other two people in the room. 'We are NOT selling this house!'

Mr Qureishi's lips pursed involuntarily.

Had I been rude? Excellent.

'Zoon . . .' Ma began. I rounded on her, rage erupting like an unattended firework.

'You just decided to *sell?* Without even asking me? Or *telling* me?'

'Zoon, it isn't like I'm not doing the right thing here . . .'

Mr Qureishi walked towards the door, speaking in a dull monotone. 'I'll give you two a minute, shall I?'

I wanted to fling him from an open window and make sure he landed on cement. But I had more pressing matters to attend to.

'Ma, the right thing? On *what level* could you *possibly* be doing the right thing?'

'Zu, keep your voice DOWN. It would be good for us to get a fresh start somewhere. We're absolutely dwarfed here; we don't seem to be *getting* anywhere. My shawls would sell better! You could go to a good school! You could see more of the world! You've hardly even seen much of Srinagar, thanks to all these curfews and restrictions! Besides, Zoon, it isn't safe for Pandits to live here any more.'

'MA! I can't believe you're saying this! We've lived here all our lives! You want to just move to some . . . some . . . *city?*'

'Now, Zu—'

'And for WHAT? What's wrong with the shawls you sell here? What's wrong with the friends we have here? I'm happy here!'

'But Zu, we could—'

'Ma, I don't *care*. I know everything you're saying may be valid. But I had a right to be *told*. IT'S MY HOME TOO!'

Encouraged by pure savagery, a nasty, spiteful little spirit born of my anger, I continued. 'I know the real reason you're selling it anyway! You just can't BEAR to be here after what happened! You think Dad's spirit is lingering here and *traumatizing* me or something! Well, the only one who's still traumatized by Dad is *you!*'

Hurt. Real hurt. Grief and pain. I could see it in her eyes. I should never have brought up what happened to Dad . . . but I couldn't stop myself. 'And besides, you'd get heaps of money, wouldn't you? Don't tell me you're doing this for me, Ma, because that's a bunch of—'

'Enough.'

She said it quietly, but there was danger behind her words, her eyes, her trembling fingers.

'You have never thought of anyone but yourself, have you, Zoon? Not even, perhaps, of poor Tathi? I suppose it has passed Your Highness's notice that she's becoming weaker and older? She needs to go to a place where she can be taken care of! Not stay here in this . . . DUMP where you can't even obtain a Band-Aid without walking half a mile! She can't live in a place like this any more! So I'd thank you to be a bit more understanding instead of being spoilt and bratty!'

'You think Tathi will agree to leave?' I shot back. 'She spent her childhood here, she got married here, she *loves* it here! You're the only one who doesn't like our house, because you never knew what it's like to grow up in it, and you're only selling it for yourself!'

'Enough, I said!' she roared, her patience finally reaching its limit. 'Zoon . . . if you can't learn how to be civil to your elders, and particularly to guests, then you can STAY UP HERE FOR THE REST OF THE EVENING!'

She slammed the door shut.

I heard her breathing slow as she thumped downstairs. She had never yelled at me like that before. Had I asked for it?

Oh, no. I had, hadn't I?

But so had she!

Their voices came muffled from behind the door, and yet their words reached me clearly enough to scald my bones.

'Er . . . all settled then?' asked Mr Qureishi, awkwardly, uninterestedly.

Her voice still shook when she spoke. 'Oh, quite all right . . . *daughters,* you know . . .'

I cringed. It hurt even more to be referred to as 'daughters'.

'Oh, yes, I quite understand. Shall we have a quick look at the exterior of the house?'

'Of course.'

I threw myself on the welcoming bed. I closed my eyes and felt the cotton grow wet under my cheek.

When I curled up in bed that night, my anger had barely evaporated; it blazed on, like an unquenchable fury that I didn't try to restrain. I was, however, getting quite drowsy, and the sheets were thick, warm and comfortable.

Deep blue light shone from the window. Occasionally the call of a shrill songbird struck shattering notes, jarring in the silence.

I looked around me at the portraits huddled up in their frames. Their beautiful colours were washed over by the dim light, but I could sense the bursting hues of their paint just underneath, like treasure buried in a shallow shore, with nothing but a watery gossamer separating it from the wind. They grunted frequently, and the long, drawn-out snoring of the king, with his crown perched lopsided on his wavy hair, was putting me to sleep.

I was a bit calmer then than I had been when I had yelled at Ma, though the thought of it sent blood coursing painfully through my veins again. But it is very difficult to be mad at someone when you're tired, and all I could do was wonder about the incident with curiosity. What was I going to do to stop the sale? And why was Ma so steadfast about selling the house anyway? Why wouldn't she listen to me? Tathi would never agree! Would she?

These thoughts and a zillion others flowed around inside my head like magma, leaving behind a tinge of anger and yet arousing my interest. They danced about drunkenly, and when they finally turned to pirates battling blue-scaled sea serpents on unknown shores and gods blessing brave warriors with enchanted arrows to slay the rakshasas, I knew I had fallen asleep.

I was dimly aware of Ma climbing into bed next to me, putting her face in her hands, and sighing deeply before laying her head on the pillow and allowing sleep to waft over her.

The next morning, when I glanced out of the window, I saw that the rain had ceased. But the clouds hung fat and heavy against the sky; it was by no means finished. The sun leaned wearily against the mountains. The valley was lush and green, a fresh coat of paint having been lovingly splashed on to it by the rain. In the distance, the light blue of a large new puddle glinted up at me merrily, unaware that soon the heat would wipe it away.

Right, I told myself sternly, there'd be no more pity parties. I had to take action. I had to take charge. I had to, to begin with, make sure everyone knew what was going on.

I glanced at the portraits. No good—they were all still asleep. Goodness, they slept something like twelve hours a day! Perhaps it was because they lived in a bedroom . . .

Ma was already up. Her sheets were tousled, tangled, twisted and utterly uncared for, thrown across her side of the bed. I straightened them, scowling. She must have gone downstairs to make herself a morning cup of kehva. Which meant that I could go sit in the library undisturbed and see if either the books or my favourite worn, cushiony black armchair had any inspiration or advice to offer with regard to the sale.

I tiptoed across the hall, leaving pillows under the sheets in case she came to check on me.

Just before entering the library, I stopped, hand on the doorknob. I had heard a most curious noise coming from—could that be right?—the walls. Now, living here, I was quite used to odd sounds, but this was entirely different. This sounded like . . . a voice. An *unfamiliar* voice. I pressed my ear to the wall where it hid, listening hard. I jumped when I heard it again, much louder then as it vibrated through the wood, like an old woman's rasp through a dense forest; I couldn't understand a word. The consonants were stretched to unrecognizability, the vowels stressed and deformed. After what seemed to me like no more than a few seconds, the walls became silent again.

Confused, I stood still for another minute, until it occurred to me that I was wasting precious time. Whatever this mystery or imagining was, it'd have to wait.

I continued on to the library.

I carefully shut the heavy wooden door behind me, pausing to make sure I didn't slam it too hard. I heard a pitter-pattering against the windows. Raining again so soon?

The books rested, quiet and peaceful, against the shelves, a deceiving air; they were so often rambunctious.

I knew that in a moment they would burst into chatter, but just then, in that moment, in that warm, cosy library, they were quietly content. They were my friends, each one of them, and they'd been keeping me company for as long as I could remember. A conversation with them brightens any day immensely. Oh, I don't suppose I've mentioned this yet, have I? Well, it's the house itself that is my closest companion, home to not just my family, but to my oldest and dearest of friends. I was not as brave as I'd have liked; I did not wish, at least not just yet, to bring them back to a cold and miserably complex reality with such alarmingly terrible news.

'Hello!' came the voice of one of the bookshelves. It was deep and rough like an elephant's, rousing his fellows. They stretched against the ceiling, as though they would burst through it at the slightest excitement. The books began to wake as well, some quickly, some excitedly and others, grumpily.

'What do you suppose I should do on such a rainy day?' I began.

'Aren't *we* quite enough for you to amuse yourself with? Honestly, you should be quite grateful you've got us at all!' said the history book crankily.

'Calm down. She's just bored,' soothed the book of Jataka Tales. 'After all, boredom is natural.'

'How about you go play in the garden? It'll give you some much-needed fresh air!' suggested Ma's gardening guide.

'Not a chance,' I replied. 'It must be a mud puddle by now.'

'Well, rain is very helpful to plants, you know, and especially good for their roots. It's so full of essential minerals, you could hardly imagine it. They're also . . .'

At the same time, the dusty notebook had begun to moan in the corner. 'Write something in me . . . something meaningful . . . all I've got inside me is a grocery list and some unfinished games of tic-tac-toe . . .'

'You know,' interrupted the fortune-teller's guide, a large, electric-blue evil eye stamped on her front, 'you seem to me to be in danger of a troubled mind.'

Ma's scrapbook of newspaper clippings began yelling something about delivering newspapers, while the book on insects chirped, 'You had a bug-catching net, didn't you? Now, where's that at?'

'Fancy a chariot race?' called the Mahabharata, while the wooden bookshelves continued to roar their unintelligence.

I couldn't get a word in until the sturdy armchair spoke in a deep, commanding voice. They all quieted down when he told them they sounded like donkeys braying for hay. Then he asked me whether the house was going to be sold or not and everyone stiffened.

The temperature in the room seemed to drop considerably, and with it, the laughter and playful sleepiness. A thick, heavy, crushing silence followed these words, as the idea of the sale turned itself over and over in my mind.

After walking over and seating myself in the armchair, I cleared my throat to speak.

For nearly a quarter of an hour I spoke into rapt silence, telling them about the stuck-up realtor and how Ma had yelled at me. The books joined in, theorizing, arguing, shouting suggestions.

The armchair ended up having to call all to order again. He hated things being out of place—he was quite like my mother in that respect—but he sorted them out in an almost fatherly fashion, so that you couldn't help but listen to him and like him for it. This was a bit funny considering he was the newest piece of furniture, added by my grandfather so he'd have a comfortable seat in the library while he read. The books often liked to joke about how much better off their lives had been when he was good and silent, and how frustrating the initial stages of his speech had been. 'We tried,' the history book was fond of saying. 'We tried to keep him quiet. But we couldn't . . . and now look at him.'

After he managed to get the books down to a soft murmur, the closest I suppose they could've got to silence under the circumstances, I spoke again.

'So of course . . . you all understand . . . we have to find a way to stop this sale. Ma isn't likely to be any help at all, as you might have guessed. We'll have to find a way to get the realtor, and his merry customers, all out of here at once.'

The books immediately erupted again. They suggested I trick him, fence him, pelt him with sticks, attack him with crystal balls, and a great many other things.

Unable to stay sombre, I laughed, not bothering to stop their clamorous bickering.

I turned around to the armchair to speak to him properly. He really was the only sensible one in this library.

'What do you think I should do?'

He was quiet for some time, considering his response as if it were his next move in a heated game of chess. 'I think there is one thing you should have done already, and it is unimaginable to me that you could've forgotten.'

'What?' I breathed.

'Go see Tathi. Go see her at once. Tell her everything. Perhaps, once she backs you up, you'll be able to put a halt to this business.'

I was so exuberant at this forgotten course of action that I could've hugged him.

'Yes! Of course! I'll go see her straight away, right after breakfast.'

'For yet another breakfast?' the armchair suggested slyly.

I giggled. Yes, that was exactly what I was thinking.

Then all at once, the armchair became pensive. His fluffy stuffing, light as cotton, seemed to grow dense within him.

'You know, they do not truly understand. Or perhaps some do, and do not wish to scare the rest. Or even you, for that matter.'

'What?'

'I'm saying that they do not all understand what will happen when this house is sold.'

'Well, you'll have to put up with some crazy strangers and I'll never see you again!'

'No.'

'What do you mean, no?'

'Your mother won't sell every piece of furniture in this house, Zoon. In fact, she's likely to keep a great deal of it. And then what will happen?'

I tried hard to focus.

'You'll all have to come with us to the . . . new house?'

'Exactly. And what will happen to us there?'

Dread sank low in my heart, searing through the rest of me, sinking within my veins, erupting in a sudden jolt of fear. It must have shown on my face, for the armchair nodded and spoke again.

'Slowly, little by little, the magic will flow out of us, just as it once flowed in. We'll die, Zoon.'

I imagined the library still.

Silent.

Empty.

'The house,' I gasped, like a bird flung through a frosty cloud, 'will die?'

The armchair paused to reflect.

'Well . . . no. The *house's* magic will be as strong as it was before we were brought here. But each of us—parts of the house, I mean—will eventually become detached from this magic.'

The heavy rain was almost sinister in its silence.

Suddenly clumsy, I blustered about, getting up, saying, 'I'm leaving right away, Tathi must be told, this is utter . . . I mean . . . it's absolute . . .'

'You think your mother will let you go out in this weather?' began the armchair.

'Without breakfast?' put in the cookbook.

'Wearing that?' giggled the fashion magazine.

A boisterous roar of laughter came from the books, the bookshelves and the armchair, and I couldn't help but grin.

'You just wait!' I chuckled. 'I'll buy you all the ugliest, thickest bookmarks in town!'

They hated bookmarks, all of them, and said that having a bookmark stuck between your pages was like having a straw jammed up your nostril—dreadfully uncomfortable. They shuddered at the thought.

The books had been right, of course. As I trooped downstairs, announcing that I was off to visit Tathi, Ma gripped me by the collar and pushed me into the chair by the desk.

'Oh, no, you don't!'

'But Ma! I need to go visit Tathi!'

'Not when it's raining as hard as this. Quit your whining and wait.'

She gave me the kind of glare that stings.

So I waited. And waited.

Ma bustled about, frequently looking over at me as though to make sure I didn't teleport out of my seat.

I stared dazedly out of the window. The world formed itself all over again with each cool drop of rain, a palette of greys used to create a masterpiece of a gentle and firm sky, almost like a mother to the quiet, muddy landscape. The drops swam down the glass of the window, merging and fusing with one another, creating tear-shaped shadows against the quill's pearl-white feather.

'Perfect for picnicking. I'm hungry,' he muttered.

I watched the dust motes beside the window float dully about, bored and lazy.

I watched the sun fight fiercely to burst through the glaze of water sheathing it.

I watched each thread of the carpet rise up to catch a piece of the blue light dancing in from the window, before shimmering back to its black and red once more.

I tuned out the chatter of the desk and chair, then arguing about whether or not pigs really could fly, and how it was all just a conspiracy against the public. They are the best of friends, but get into frightfully trivial and tiring quarrels. Though I must say, in this case, the desk had a fair point.

At last, the rain began to thin, easing first into a light shower, and finally, into a drizzle so fine you might not have noticed it if you were wearing a hat. Leaping up from my chair as though pricked by a pin, I flung open the door. I heard Ma click her tongue impatiently, but she hadn't made to physically restrain me in any way, and I took that as a sign to leave before she changed her mind.

I patted the bark of the chinar, just to say good morning. It hummed pleasantly under my fingers, life beneath rough, firm wood.

It was pleasantly cool. Before closing the gate, I snatched a small cherry from one of the trees in our garden. I bit into it, and tasted the rain. It was a perfect blend of crunchy, sour, sweet and fresh. I shut the gate behind me.

It became a little frostier—as it always does—when I walked out, but I was well used to that feeling by then. I began my march towards Tathi's house. She lives at Dal Gate, closer to the lakeside.

The trees wafted gently in the breeze, a bright orange leaf often coming to rest at my feet. They looked like a towering wall of a thousand suns, each burning brighter than its neighbour. I crossed a sudden break in the shade, momentarily exposed to the sky, so that a raindrop splashed down on my nose, and autumn's chill seemed to seep through my warm blue cotton shirt, icy and reviving against my skin.

I waved as I passed the chana stand, its posts teetering dangerously, its surface scraped to near scrap, its tilting sign left with nothing but a single, faded C. The chana vendor waved back. To me, his greetings are as refreshing as the crunch of the snacks he sells. He's a bit on the short side, his limbs verging on chubby, his smile crooked as his workplace, his brown hair giving way to sudden flashes of white, betraying that his years here have taken their toll. I have never known his name, but whenever I pass I wave, and he waves back. It's a sort of code between us, a secret we take childish joy in sharing, our oasis of undeclared unity in these deserted streets.

My chappals squelched noisily against the muddy dirt road. A few miles ahead, I could see the first military check post, barbed wire against its pointed tip and soggy footprints made by heavy boots on every side. A man sat rigidly within it, unsmiling, clutching at the handle of a large, heavy automatic as though it were a part of him. A large red sign extended from the edge of the post, slicing Kashmir in half.

I scowled. These horrid posts did disturb the view. Around back, I heard noises of a commotion. An old man, his hands wrinkled and twisted nearly to the point of being broken, was protesting weakly as he was shoved in the chest by a tough, gruff military guard whose neck was the width of my whole body. Their voices were garishly loud and laced with growing fury. I hurried along. I'd seen this too times before, and I didn't want to be around when those boys with filthy handkerchiefs tied roughly around their matted hair and hollow cheeks arrived. I did not want to watch as they began throwing stones at the military men, their eyes wild with the unquenchable flame of vengeance. I didn't want to be around when the men fought back with unceasing gunfire, and Kashmiri boys fell to the ground, clutching an arm, a knee, a chest.

The sound of lapping water began to grow clearer.

Soon I crossed the corner of the road, humming to myself, and saw the lane that led to Tathi's house. It was almost hidden by prickly bushes, and I often thought that at one time, when she was healthier and did not have the pain in her knee, she would come out and push them aside, inviting people in. I pressed past them, a single thorn grazing my right thigh, before I managed to trip on to the soft-soiled lane leading to Tathi's. The gentle orange light danced playfully before me, and I looked up at the canopy of tangerine trees forming a sanctuary in the small path of Srinagar. Her house lay cosily sunken into the ground, latticed windows flung wide open to catch the wind. Behind it, glints of deep blue lake water shone through gaps in the trees.

Once I reached the door, an old, worn thing of light brown wood, I knocked exactly four times, counted to five, and then knocked once again. That was the signal; now that she knew it was me, she'd open the door. We'd come up with this after a young girl had badgered her for a week, trying to get her to buy a walking stick. It reached its peak when she invited herself in and began setting up shop in the living room.

Moments later, Tathi flung open the door, a beaming smile across her face, her thick, round glasses planted firmly on her nose. Her soft, black eyes gleamed brightly as ever, filling me with a familiar glow, and I always expected to see a scattering of stars within them. She pulled me into a warm yet crushing hug. I tried hard to get my arms around her, but I couldn't, of course, as usual. She was as squat and round as the thick, white bun upon her head. As we trooped in, I took in the smell of a spicy curry mixed with the warmth of a motherly fire and the chill of the sneaky air that had rushed in playfully while the door had been open.

'Ah,' I murmured softly, throwing myself into the beanbag by the fire. Tathi had made it for me on my ninth birthday out of an old bed sheet and some dried peas from the market. She came to join me in her rocking chair, and asked me how my birthday prep was going. I let my feet press against the heated marble of the fireplace as we chatted and laughed.

Without warning, the sound of gunshots came as clearly through the walls as if the bullets had gone straight through them. The unmistakable animalistic roars of a mob followed, their demands for freedom and equality and blood ringing sharply through the room, declaring, as always, that the humiliation had gone on long enough.

This one seemed different from the others, though . . . much closer somehow. I thought of the fight I'd seen on the way there, and how it had done me good to hurry. I felt disgustedly angry and sickened for a moment, as I always did, but neither Tathi nor I seemed to think that speaking of what was occurring outside would make it any better.

We paused briefly, then pressed on, determined not to let anything intrude on our bliss.

Tathi chuckled that I'd put on weight. Grinning, I admitted having dreamt about her rogan josh, and she laughed while poking me in the belly and saying that my father and I were just the same.

Eventually, I could no longer keep the sale away from my mind. It had been eating away at our conversation, a gluttonous maggot, until it was pushing against the inside of my heated forehead, bursting to be acknowledged.

But where should I start?

I waited for that familiar lull in the conversation when a joke has just been told or a memory just relived, before beginning.

'Tathi, there's something I came to tell you about.'

'Yes, Zuzu?'

'It's a rather upsetting thing to say, so I just kept putting it off, but I really can't any more.'

Outside, the rain had stopped, and the afternoon slept tiredly against the valley, drowsy from the downpour.

'Ma has decided to sell the house.'

Tathi's smile seemed to shrink until her lips were pressed together. Her eyes flickered away, painfully thoughtful.

'She didn't tell me. I didn't know till the realtor arrived,' I went on.

'The realtor?' Her eyes flashed.

'Yes. His name is Mr Qureishi. He came to see the house yesterday, and he's frightfully superior and smug.'

'Did he say who would be buying it?'

I looked up at her. She looked worried, certainly, and quite out of sorts, but I had expected her to be as enraged as I'd been.

'Well, no one, if we have any say in it!'

She stared at me.

'Well, we can't just let someone *buy* it! They would *die*!'

I bit my lip ruefully, realizing what I'd said. I didn't know if Tathi had ever spoken to any of my friends. She hardly ever came over to our house. And I'd given up telling people about them after that disastrous attempt when I was six. I had tried my best to get Chandani Auntie to speak with the fireplace, and to see why I found him so likeable. But she'd merely stared at him blankly despite my warm introductions and his (unusually quiet) greeting. She had later had a talk with me about imaginary and real friends. I'd asked the fireplace why he'd remained so stoic and silent, and his answer was that he was 'really disinclined to speak with such a dislikeable woman'. I didn't attempt to introduce her to any more of them, or even speak to them in front of anybody again after that. I didn't need her or anyone else thinking I was cuckoo.

But was I? I didn't know. I'd been speaking with them for as long as I could remember. They were my family, weren't they? I couldn't just let them go!

Tathi interrupted my twisted whirlpool of thoughts, in which our conversation, a rotted old sailboat, had caught and been dragged to the depths.

'Who would die, Zuzu?'

'Um . . . well . . . you and me! Or me, at least. I couldn't leave our house, Tathi! I couldn't leave Kashmir!'

She smiled. It was a bit too knowing.

'I know. Neither could I. I would always wish to remain with the scented, flowery wind . . . the soft blossoms and shikaras of spring . . . the fires of winter . . . the leaves of autumn . . . the mountain range to marvel at each sunrise . . . the snow, gentle as a kiss, blanketing the year's failures underneath fresh beauty . . . oh, I could never live anywhere else.'

It was my turn then to break her reverie.

'Exactly. So we can't just let the house get sold, can we? Can I tell Ma you've said that? She said we had to move because you were getting old, but I *told* her you'd never choose to leave.'

Tathi gave me a curious, unsmiling glance. She thought for a little longer than a moment before saying, 'Yes, you tell your mother that. Tell her that I surely cannot leave. And I don't know . . . if you . . . hmmm . . .'

I stared at her. What was she talking about? *Cannot* leave? Why wasn't she meeting my eye? Where had her smile gone? Where had her wits gone?

She leapt up suddenly, as though trying to negate what had just happened.

'Well, after that piece of news, I should think you'd want some leftover yakhni from last night! I shall get it right away!'

And she bustled off towards the kitchen, her hands clasped tight together.

The rain had stopped entirely by the time I walked back home. I squelched my feet alternately through each puddle

I came across on the mud-soaked streets. Occasionally, I came across one with a bit of dark red, which I surmised was blood, so I did not step in those. I passed the banks of a small tributary of Dal Lake, the water still and quiet. I waved at those I passed, who were few and deadened, and did not wave back. The chana stand was empty, a few grimy wrappers sliming across its wood.

Lameeya Auntie was tending the few wisps of garden left to her, and waved as I passed. I smiled in return, wondering vaguely about Altaf. The houses lay mellow and silent, hidden within the valley.

Finally, I reached the old, worn gate of my home. I rushed inside, eager to warm my chattering teeth and chilled bones. My eyes flicked towards the chinar as I felt my limbs grow warmer inside my frosty shirt. And that's when it first hit me. The dull auric tree was looking . . . well, not smaller—I knew that was impossible—but sick somehow, as though it didn't really feel like standing up as straight as before. As though it *couldn't*. My feet had gone on without my mind, and before I could think through the thing properly, I was at the door. Labelling it as another product of this dreary day, I pushed it open.

As soon as I entered, taking off my chappals near the umbrella, Ma came over with a lit diya and a bit of halwa in our metal *tambri*.

'For Puranmashi,' she murmured as she passed me some halwa.

The atmosphere began to uncoil itself as she fed me. My anger at her seemed to soften at the edges. The fireplace murmured a sleepy welcome from the living room. I accepted a bit of warm halwa from her hands, and it melted delightfully on my tongue, leaving me with the gentle, cosy contentment of home.

We walked over to the small clay figurine of Kheer Bhawani Mata, once in a deep red sari with long, black hair and a powerful chakra in her left hand, then chipped horribly at the sides so that it no longer resembled a god so much as a mound of putty. Ma began aarti, and softly sang a mountain prayer, formed long ago in the winds of the hills, the pulse of Kashmir beating loudly through the music.

I couldn't sleep. My stomach seemed intent on lurching, as though at sea, my brain set on providing as many reminders as possible of how little I'd accomplished in the way of stopping the sale. Finally, sick at heart, I began to turn slowly in bed, moving like the hands of a clock, slipping my bare, chilled feet into my too-large chappals and leaving my mother in bed.

Every step I took down the stairs seemed to echo in the gathering black. Ah, what a relief it was when I leapt down the last couple of stairs and saw the enchanted living room, bathed in moonlight, shimmering in the deep blue velvet of night.

All was silent, the carpet muffling not only my steps but also the fury of the thoughts within me, so that I felt distinctly calm as I moved towards the fireplace.

My wrist flicked involuntarily, and I heard the window give a slight rattle. I turned towards it, curious, and twisted my wrist again, but this time, it did not move. The wind, I supposed. Ma had brought in fresh wood that morning. Its scent, warm and comforting, drifted about the living room.

I had expected the fireplace, despite his age, to wake up excitedly as soon as I hopped down next to him. But he stayed asleep, snoring loudly, shifting the small piles of ash every now and then, his crest quivering with every breath. I poked him hard, a decidedly difficult task to accomplish, given that he was marble. He grunted, began to mutter something about radishes, then became still again.

'Wake up!' I hissed.

'Hmm? What's happened?'

'We need to talk, log-head!'

'Oh . . . yes . . . I'm sure . . . it's just . . . the quill's been waking me up so many . . . many times . . . to tell me . . . his vague . . . philosophies . . . but . . . oh, yes. Happy . . . happy birthday, Zoons . . .'

I stared at him incredulously, and then kicked him as quietly as I could manage. My toe hurt terribly.

'What? What?'

'My birthday isn't for two days! Now wake UP, you worthless thing, WAKE UP!'

'All right, all right, I'm up!'

'The house is going to be sold.'

'Hmm?'

'This house is going to be sold.'

'Oh . . . that's nice, Zoon . . . okay . . .'

He gave a great sigh, his mixed murmurs becoming incoherent once more.

My irritation bubbled over. I picked up a beautiful, freshly cut log from the fireplace.

'Hey . . . what're you doing to . . . that's my best log!'

'What? This mangy old thing?'

'Yes. THAT MANGY OLD THING. Drop it!'

'No. It will stay in my lap until you listen to me, do you understand?'

The fireplace huffed irritably, then alert.

'Did you hear what I said? About the house being . . . sold?'

'SOLD?' the fireplace roared, his slightly croaky voice growing even hoarser as he did so, spluttering a little on his ashes. I rolled my eyes. It always takes a while to get his fire going. 'Who's selling it? Why? Where will I stay? Where will YOU stay?'

'Calm down and be quiet! Ma's asleep!'

Suddenly a silence fell upon us.

'What?' I whispered.

The fireplace was still for a second too long.

'Nothing. So what's up with this sale?'

I stared at him for a moment, and then continued briskly, 'Well, Ma wants the house to be sold, for some unfathomable reason. She didn't even ASK ME what I thought, before she called the realtor over to our house as though he was her long-lost childhood friend or something . . .'

'A realtor? What did he say?'

'Not much, just that he'd be glad to sell and that we already had a few potential buyers.'

'Of course, he's going to make a lot of money. Glad to sell . . .' the fireplace muttered darkly. We sat in an angry silence. My teeth tugged fiercely at the inside of my cheek. 'And he said there are already a few people interested in the house?'

I nodded gravely, all hope dampening.

'But if no one has actually been determined yet . . . Hmm . . . this could work . . . You see, if there are *many* potential buyers, then, from what I remember, each one of them will probably want to come over to see the house, right?'

I groaned. I hadn't even thought of it. 'Oh, yes, that's right. They probably will. Ugh! I couldn't bear it! That stuck-up realtor . . . We *have* to do something!'

'I know! Exactly my point! So, I think I've come up with a way to keep them out.'

I stared sceptically. The fireplace, despite being the oldest member of the house, often had these strange ideas that needed to be burnt out of him.

'If you're talking about barricading the gate or something—'

'No, no. Just listen. For the next couple of days, I think you should go about making the house as dirty as you can.'

'Dirty?'

'Absolutely filthy.'

I stared at the fireplace as though he'd finally lost one log too many.

'Morning everyone,' the quill interrupted. 'My gosh! Have you seen the size of that eclipse?'

Ignoring him entirely, I replied, 'Why would I do that?'

'Your mother will only invite people to see the house if it's clean and pretty and, well, sellable! She won't call them till she thinks the house is tidy enough,' the fireplace explained.

It began to dawn on me, slowly, like the mist of a rising sun in the haze of winter.

'I'd use a telescope, but I find they're not reliable at the best of times. No, I met one once that told me I'd come from the head of an eagle. Completely inaccurate, of course; I come from the mane of a unicorn.'

I pressed on.

'So if the house is never clean enough to show them . . .'

'Then they never come to see it, and hopefully they never buy it either,' the fireplace finished, pausing for a moment to cough up some ash.

I thought for a minute. It wasn't a bad plan. It seemed logical, and not too grand or convoluted. Perhaps a few buyers may become disinterested.

'It wouldn't stop her indefinitely.'

'Of course not. But it would buy us time.'

I was silent. Time . . . with which to convince Ma that this wasn't the right path. With which to get Tathi on my side. With which to find a way to get that realtor out of here permanently.

'Make sure you go visit Tathi when you can,' the fireplace interjected, disrupting my tumble of thoughts.

'I already did,' I responded dully. 'She didn't help as much as I thought she would. But on the bright side, she did say she'd never leave here.'

'That's a start,' said the fireplace encouragingly, and his embers brightened like flakes of gold amidst the deep brown of the wood, lighting up the crest.

'Shocking, I know. But you know what they say! "Once a unicorn, never a leprechaun,"' quoted the quill.

I yawned, so long and loud that I felt my eyes begin to water with fatigue. My thoughts drifted vaguely to a soft, cosy bed and mornings spent sleeping in, dreaming to the sound of the rain.

I put the log carefully back into the fireplace. I'd never admit it to him—I might lose a valuable bargaining chip—but I cared about the beauty of his flames just as much as he did. I'd never truly have the guts to damage his wood.

'Goodnight!' he whispered.

With steps as silent as a ghost ship gliding amongst the waves, I swept upstairs. I took one last look at the moon, seemingly full yet riddled with craters like a round of cheese, before leaping into bed and letting my eyes slip shut. A wave of stillness washed over me before another thought could enter my mind.

Chapter Four

My eyelids fluttered open. The sun was rising like a phoenix, shining light over the darkened countryside. I turned over and went back to sleep.

When morning finally came, it brought with it a great sense of purpose. I brushed my teeth with unnecessary force and grim determination while staring, unfocused, out of the foggy window. Shankaracharya Hill was barely visible, even from this distance. Impatiently, I ran a hand over its glass—I couldn't recall a time when it had ever been this distorted. I longed for the sight of the baby-blue sky, flushed with activity, clouds mischievously twirling around the steady mountains. It was a sight that brought beauty in its simplicity, and in its need for nothing but unspoken happiness.

The first thing to do, I decided, was to make sure everyone was fully briefed on our course of action, so that it could be carried out with the utmost efficiency.

I knocked sharply on the frame of each portrait in the bedroom, causing their inhabitants to grumble sleepily.

The Mughal warrior opened his eyes at once when I reached him. He seemed to have been on the alert all night. For a moment, he peered at me questioningly. Then, as though something had flashed red-hot against the inside of his temple, he started.

'The house! The realtor! What are we planning to do?'

I waited until he had ceased his frantic muttering of various prayers, interspaced by the snores and snorts of the kisan, before continuing.

I filled him in with short, quick, hushed sentences. Slowly, his eyes hardened and shone with a sense of pride and duty. 'I'll wake the others,' he said. 'You tell the rest.'

I opened the closet and dressed hurriedly. All at once, a shiny dress crammed into Ma's side of the closet caught my eye. It was the salwar she'd worn to greet the realtor. And the tear at the side was gaping wider than ever. I frowned, and patted the side of the closet. Shouldn't it have been mended by now? Anyhow, I was in such a rush I couldn't be bothered to investigate.

The books had taken rather longer to come on board, given that they were so full of thoughts and words that it was difficult to cram in any more. Indeed, I only managed it with a great deal of help from the armchair, who'd predictably been the first to understand. At first, I hadn't been able to get them to quiet down until I'd stamped my foot out of frustration. That seemed to cut instantly through their blabber, as though ripples of silence had burst forth from the spot where my foot touched the ground. This was something to be marvelled at; they normally never listened to me.

Halfway down the stairs, I stopped. There was something heavy and nauseating, like a small toad, in my belly. The air around me tasted oddly lifeless, seemingly carrying a sickness. My eyes darted around; every surface was immobile and quiet.

I shivered, my body attempting to throw off the feeling, and pulled down the sleeves of my top.

Something was wrong.

I bit my lip. This warranted attention. Would the armchair know what was going on? I turned to move upstairs once more—and froze, my foot on the upper step; I'd heard the fireplace call out my name.

Letting out a small puff of air, I told myself to concentrate on this sale. Anything else, I assured my troubled mind, could wait for later; I must deal with the urgent matters first, and hurry.

Once I reached downstairs, I found, thankfully, that the fireplace had already told the desk and chair. They seemed to be caught in the throes of yet another serious debate, and I was glad not to have to explain something of such importance to either of them.

There was no point telling the quill, who was currently dozing in his inkpot. Half the time I wasn't sure whether he was even aware of me speaking to him. Fondly, I recalled the time when he'd told me my hair smelled like almonds in spring.

'Zoons?' Ma's voice came from the living room. At first, I smiled. Then, as though ice, rather than rain, had fallen from the sky, I felt myself grow sharp and cold.

'What, Ma?'

I saw her come slowly into view from the doorway and lean against the banister. She seemed surprised at my tone. 'Nothing, Zu, I just wanted to know what you'd like for breakfast. I've made—'

'I'm not really hungry.'

As cutting as it sounded, it was true. All of a sudden, I'd lost all desire for food.

Ma pursed her lips. 'Fine.'

She moved towards the cooking range, and I heard something creak loudly beneath her feet, below the carpet. My brow furrowed at the unusual noise. To me, it sounded like a rusty knife grating against a metal plate.

My nose caught a passing whiff of saag, as though it had been trying to shrink itself down and escape before I smelled it. I turned towards Ma, who was adding a spoonful of cumin seeds into the mix over the stove.

'Why are you making saag?'

'Because.' Her voice sounded coarse, clipped.

'Because what?'

'We're going to be having some visitors today.'

'Chandani Auntie again? She'll be happy to see any food . . .'

'No, Zoon. You don't know them.'

'Then why are they coming?'

The toad in my stomach was taking broad, clumsy leaps.

'They're coming to see the house. Along with Mr Qureishi. And unless you are sure that you've the capacity to behave, you may wait upstairs for the duration of their visit. Understand?'

I stood stock-still, shocked. She'd invited them already? It was then that I noticed a few folded chairs against the fridge beside her, borrowed, I supposed, from Chandani Auntie, and the extra cutlery lined up near the stove, no doubt unearthed from various drawers and unused cupboards.

'Zoon. I said, do you understand?'

'Yes.'

The word emerged muffled, struggling to pass through gritted teeth.

'Good.'

I watched her chop up a deep green pepper, riddled with seeds, and sprinkle it on the saag. Its smell wafted leisurely across the room, not bothering to hide itself. Rather, it spread enticingly past each door left ajar, swirling through hidden corners, making my nostrils widen at the scent of seasoned spinach and greens.

I glanced towards the fireplace through the doorway to the living room to see how he felt about such a discouraging development, and immediately noticed that he was subtly crushing his logs against his sides, so that they splintered and grew rough. Perhaps it was the way the light hit him, but his crest was almost invisible. I gasped, and then turned towards the door.

The top of the desk seemed to be shifting ever so slightly to catch grey spots of dust swirling in the sunlight. His surface was growing steadily filthier as he did so, as was the oblivious quill's greying feather.

My gaze turned to fix on the chair. He was muttering encouragement to the desk under his breath. And yet he looked a little too clean himself . . .

All at once, acting on pure instinct, I twisted my wrist with my hand pointed towards the chair's wooden leg.

I was nowhere near enough to touch him, and yet he moved along with my wrist, contorting until it looked like he might crack under the slightest weight. Startled, I stared down at my palms; I'd never been able to do that before. The chair did not seem to have noticed, yet he looked as though someone enormous had sat on him too hard.

Well, whatever had just occurred, it had helped me immensely.

With a lurch, I moved towards the living room. In a small corner of the room was a drawer in which Ma kept the cleaning supplies. Judging by the visible sheen of grey atop it, she hadn't yet begun to spruce up the house for the visitors' arrival. 'Hurry!' whispered the fireplace, and I nodded hard, moving quicker.

Pulling out the red cloth that we always used to dust, I pressed it to the dirtiest part of the carpet. I pulled it away and saw, satisfied, that it had turned a shade darker. Perfect.

Next, I reached for the bottom of the drawer and found the shaggy *jhaadu*. I was normally the one who swept the house, since it gave Ma a backache. It was already so old I couldn't think of what to do to make it any less effective, so I finally settled on yanking out a few of its long jute strands. Just then, more of its fibres sailed unbidden into my palm, as though my hand were a magnet to them. I frowned, trying to make sense of it.

Hearing Ma's footsteps, I slammed the drawer shut and ran upstairs. When I entered the bedroom, my jaw hit the ground, smashed through it and continued to fall. The sheets had sprawled themselves across the floor, the bed had more wrinkles in its fabric than Tathi's forehead and every painting not only seemed faded and dull, but was also tilted ludicrously to the side.

'What do you think?' trilled the empress, twirling in her grimy frame as if showing off a new dress. 'Most of it was my idea, of course.'

I nodded quickly, unable to speak. There was no way she'd bring them to see the bedroom now! It seemed as though embittered, shrunken demons had gnawed, slapped and scraped at everything with their long, sharp claws. I moved back into the library, where I was greeted with a similar sight. Each book stood crooked in the bookshelf, and I had arrived just in time to see a final few leap around and switch places with each other, so that colours, sizes and genres clashed to make a mixed jumble of books within a maze of shelves. The armchair seemed to have puffed himself out to the point of bursting. He looked fat and uncomfortable, his springs pressing against his surface and attempting to erupt right out.

I shut the door, silently euphoric at the effort my friends had put in despite the twinge of guilt at how Ma would attempt frantically to put everything right again. But it was better to keep the house and cost Ma a bit of effort than to lose something so irreplaceable. Besides, it was her own fault—she'd decided to sell the house in the first place, and hadn't even bothered to ask me about it!

It was almost appalling how pleased the realtor was with Ma's saag. I supposed he was too dim-witted to figure out how to make some himself. While he slurped at the saag like a skinny, sly lizard, Ma listened eagerly to his comments on where they were with the sale.

I stood in the doorway, trying to see if his glossy, gelled hair would deflate and slump against his scalp if I stared hard enough.

'Well, it is most surprising, but out of the three potential buyers, only one can be here today. I had been under the notion that all three had agreed to come, but one of them sent word yesterday to say he had a crisis at work, and another phoned me not a moment ago to say he wouldn't be free for a while, on account of his son's injury. It is most curious . . .'

He stared into the distance, frowning, and then shook his head as though startled by a fly.

'Anyhow, these days, you simply can't count on people to be punctual. Not regular, you know? Never keep to time.'

Ma was nodding vigorously, showing most plainly that she agreed with his every word. As far as I could remember, she'd never showed up on time for anything in her life.

I shared a disgusted look with the desk, who, unfortunately, was serving as a makeshift table for the two of them.

The doorbell sounded. Ma flung the door open even as she plastered a delighted smile across her face.

There, standing at our doorstep, was a most repulsive man. He was short and squat, with dark, beady eyes, and hair so unnaturally white that he appeared ill. Behind him, the sky twisted and thundered as a troubled sea. A leaf, faded and yellowing, trailed through the air behind him, landing dejectedly against rough soil. It couldn't have been the chinar's, though. Our chinar never sheds.

He stepped in and the door immediately slammed shut behind him, as though it had been fighting to close against Ma's grip.

Ma wasted no time in decking the doorway with rose petals for his arrival. Once she had finished introducing herself and trilling on about how happy she was to have him visit, she pulled me forward for a similar performance.

'And this here is my daughter, Zoon!'

'How nice.'

'Zoon, this is Mr Bhukhari.'

I stood like a dummy, my smile tight and closed. Predictably, that was not near enough for Ma.

'Zu, don't you want to say hello?'

I gritted my teeth.

For the first time since this man had arrived, I looked right into his eyes.

That was my first mistake.

His eyes were dark holes of storming, pitch black, forcing an icy, shuddering cold into my soul. They scuttled over his face, seemingly multiplying and ensnaring me in a silken cocoon of anguish and despair. Hopelessness surged through me, disrupting the idle thoughts of a simpler morning.

I tore myself from his shattering gaze. Horrified, I looked away.

'Nice to meet you . . .' The words stumbled from my mouth, my confident airs and graces tripping over a stone jutting out fiercely from the pavement.

Despite the gentle drizzle against the windows, his skin was utterly parched, as if it had all but evaporated before it touched him. A smile slithered over the corners of his cracked lips. 'Oh, the pleasure's all mine.'

Ma smiled, pleased at this show of goodwill.

She busied herself with pouring four cups of noon chai she knew I didn't like.

My eyes, once shining with superiority, never left the carpet.

But it mattered little; no more words were expected of me. Mr Bhukhari was seated and handed some chai. More saag, accompanied by hot pakoras, was promptly served. And talk of the sale began slipping into idle conversation until, like parasites, it grew to lord over the table.

'Yes, I am *very* pleased with the look of the house. I've hardly any changes I'd want to make,' barked Mr Bhukhari, bringing the chai to his lips.

'Oh, that's wonderful!' simpered Ma. I threw up a little in my mouth. *What* had happened to her? 'And you know, we are so honoured to be selling it to such a respected politician!'

Yes, so honoured. So very honoured. Utterly and completely bursting with the honour.

'So,' put in the realtor in a business-like fashion, 'when would we be ready to sign papers for the sale? You know, of course, Mrs Razdan, that before we sell we'd need to call in some professionals to . . . clean it up.' His eyes lingered on the desk and the chair, which were looking dusty, creaky and ready to collapse at a moment's notice. I smiled to myself. He continued briskly, 'That, I presume, should take at least a week or so. And I would need to, of course, review the contract with the both of you and ensure you both agree with its terms. Then we'd need to go over taxes and the like.'

Ma nodded a bit too fast, like a schoolboy fighting to give the impression of comprehension. 'Oh, sure, we'll have all that done. Immediately.'

'I'll be ready to buy it as soon as possible,' said Mr Bhukhari.

'And we'll be ready to sell it as soon as possible!' said Ma.

I winced as fake laughter swarmed upwards from their throats.

I had started a shop, got married, grown old and left all I had to my children by the time Mr Bhukhari was done seeing the house. He had stopped and peered at each object, commented on every thread of the carpet and questioned each grain of white in the wood. Though at first I'd been pleased to see how the dust and clutter in the house was making him uncomfortable, by the time they reached the library, I had collapsed by the fireplace from boredom.

Finally, Ma was ushering them out of the door. Mr Bhukhari wasn't smiling, and I took that to mean that our attempts at sabotaging the sale had worked. But then again, from what I'd seen of him, he hardly ever smiled. The realtor said something about further visitors while adjusting his hat for the final time. The door closed behind the two of them with a satisfying thump.

Ma gave a great sigh, presumably because her cheeks had grown exhausted from keeping that horrid smile in place that long.

'So,' she began, and I was relieved to hear her voice had returned to its reasonable self, 'I was thinking maybe we should go out today, do something fun.'

I paused. 'Why?'

'Well, Zoons, I just think I haven't seen a lot of you lately. And maybe we need some time to sort things out between us.'

She reached over and patted my head. It felt like hot chocolate was radiating through her palm and into me. I smiled without meaning to.

'All right. Where do you want to go?'

My excitement responded before she could, as though a jack-in-the-box of childish happiness had burst open inside me. 'Oh, let's go for a shikara ride! Please?'

She beamed.

'And we could buy some strawberries . . . and mushrooms . . .'

'It isn't even strawberry season!'

'We might find some!'

'You're hungry again, aren't you?'

We laughed.

It had taken us a while to reach the lake, given our leisurely stroll and idle chatter. We'd stopped once or twice along the way, having seen Rani Auntie near one of the local temples and tarrying to ask her whether she'd like to come along. She'd shivered through a shake of her head, bundled carefully in her yellow shawl; the wind didn't agree with her much.

Now that we were there, my nose had gone slightly red, my eyes glistening with the cold, and I, too, was bundled up like a jalebi so that my smiling mouth was hidden beneath a thick scarf. The weather seemed to have worsened. The sky was dark and heavy, hiding the sun, and the clouds hung down like clusters of poisonous grapes. A few raindrops smacked down on us, fat, frosty and unpleasant.

Shankaracharya Hill, once a grand, motherly figure against the landscape of Kashmir, was engulfed by grey fog that clung to its surface like suffocating gas.

The water was black and thick like oil, splashing noisily against the cracked rocks on the bank. The shikaras clinked gently against one another, like the last few coins inside the small, frayed pouches of their owners.

The cherry trees were few and bare, sprinkled around the blackened stone. I pined for their pink blossoms drifting gently across the clear water.

A little way off, the hawkers croaked out pleas to passers-by, flinging up dented necklaces, splintering carvings, last hopes. Their tired legs sat rough and unused against bits of cloth, the only thing shielding them from the filth of the bumpy road. Their eyes had receded into their wrinkled faces, exhausted and hopeless from all they'd been made to see.

A short distance up ahead, a starving stray, his belly a concave hollow, sniffed hopefully at a dead leaf as it landed beside his paw.

Ma made her way to the shikara owners, her dupatta catching on a stone as she went, so that she nearly stumbled over towards them. She made to ask them in swift Hindi as to how much one ride would cost. I recognized her tone to be the one she used when bargaining for salwars and the like.

'Sorry, ma'am. *Aaj toh koi bhi nahin ja raha hai.* No one going now.'

Ma turned to me, a disappointed look on her face.

'None of them will take us out right now, Zoon. The weather is too harsh.'

As if to punctuate her point, a disgustingly large raindrop splattered against my forehead.

We trooped back home in silence, drained and cold. Even the hot, fresh handful of chana we bought on the way back, accompanied by a jibe about the rain from the unusually pallid chana man, did little to nudge my lips to break into a smile; I barely contributed to the conversation as Ma congratulated him on becoming a father. Each step echoed how little I wanted to return; Ma was sure to begin cleaning out the rooms or arranging to meet electricians, painters and plumbers to see how quickly they could finish work. I knew this because she was not the sort of person to leave a task unfinished or half done, even for a moment.

As we started on the familiar road to our house, a few gulaals dangling off Lameeya Auntie's balcony caught my eye. The insides were black as a bee's stripes, and the petals appeared as deep red wine dripping from its centre.

All at once, I was struck by a very persuasive idea. Acting on impulse, I turned quickly to Ma.

'Ma, can I go visit Altaf instead?'

She peered at me, surprised.

'Just because, you know, I was all excited about coming out, and now we can't go out on the lake so . . .'

She blinked once, then nodded.

'Okay. Sure. But do you really want to, Zoon? I mean, you never showed any particular liking for him when you met.'

'Oh, but I'd only just seen him then. I want to get to know him better. And I'd love to visit Lameeya Auntie and Bhasharat Uncle!'

A small sigh escaped her lips.

'All right. Don't be back late, don't break anything, and remember your manners.'

'Iwillgreatthanksbye!'

Before she could say anything else, I did a quick U-turn and zipped back down the road towards Altaf's house.

Chapter Five

I saw him in front of the house, scattering a few flowers across the doorstep. Lameeya Auntie had often told me that this was good luck. He was going about it rather grumpily, though, tossing the flowers over each other; I supposed he hadn't been given a choice. His white cap was pulled thin like a second skin across his skull. The gate leaned tiredly against the grass, too exhausted to be welcoming as it once was. Faded scratches in its wood proclaimed the family name—Ali.

Their house had often given me the impression of a sweet old woman in a rocking chair, knitting a scarf for a son who'll never come home.

Small bits of jumbled wet cloth had been thrown over balconies meshed at odd edges of the house. Two of the four windows had been thrown open, their lattices forming twisted patterns of daylight, and a light hum of chatter could be heard from within.

Altaf's room was so easily picked out from the line-up; a jumble of small stones were scattered across the dusty windowsill, accompanied by a small wax statue of a cricket player, chipped at the edges so that it shone in the sunlight. The desk whose corner peeked out from the window was littered with crumpled paper and one battered notebook, open to a page displaying rough, hurried pencil marks woven neatly together.

I cleared my throat and Altaf looked up. He smiled when he saw me, chores forgotten, a smile that I was surprised to find myself fully return as he came bobbing over. It seemed he was half full of helium; he could never quite remain firmly on the ground.

'Hi! What's up?' he asked as he neared me.

'Oh, nothing much. I just thought I'd come over and say hello.'

'Sure! Do you want to come in?' For a moment, I hesitated. It had been all well and good to tell my own mother that I'd go visit, but now that the moment was truly upon me it seemed a bit awkward to be bursting into someone's home like that. I'd only been to Lameeya Auntie's house a few times before, that too when neither of her sons were home. Heck, I hadn't even *known* Altaf properly until a few days earlier. He was nice enough, and I had taken a liking to his buoyant and ditzy nature, but I didn't know if I was welcome to invite myself over whenever it suited me. Really, this seemed like a worse and worse idea with every word I uttered.

Altaf obviously noticed my discomfort.

'You don't really HAVE to come in . . . I just thought . . . do you want to . . . um . . . play hopscotch instead?'

He gestured to small chalk markings against the pavement to the side of the house. Illegible markings—once numbers, presumably—had been scrawled roughly within haphazard blocks.

Had I been slightly younger and more impulsive, I might have let escape a loud noise of disgust. I had never truly been one for hopscotch; I hated anything that got me sweaty or muddy for no discernible reason.

'Oh . . . no . . . I don't think so . . . I don't really . . . play hopscotch.'

'All right. Maybe we could go riding instead?'

I had been on the verge of calling the whole thing off when his final suggestion beckoned me to reconsider.

'Well . . . why not . . . but . . . it's still raining,' I responded weakly.

'It's only a drizzle! Come on, let's get the horses.'

He gripped my wrist and bounded off, dragging me with him. We stomped around the small vegetable patch bordering the side of the house and emerged some ways behind it, and I caught sight of a small path twisting backwards from the house. I'd visited the stables often—far more often than even their house—but never travelled this path before.

So we set off, speaking of things that, in truth, matter very little, but in conversation, matter a great deal. He told me he liked drawing. I told him I liked reading. And neither of us understood the other, yet somehow, we came closer together. On the way, Altaf leapt up to snatch an apple from his neighbour's tree, chuckling that it was fair game because the apple had been hanging over the fence. Within minutes, we'd reached the small open space where Altaf's father kept his horses.

I saw Bhasharat Uncle in the very middle of the clearing, speaking loudly and gruffly with another man. Bhasharat Uncle was a tough old man, who'd known war more than once. His knuckles were scraped and rough like leather, his moustache was matted and untidy, sprawled out over his lip, and his belly stood as a growing testament to his age. His eyes still shone brightly whenever he spoke, and he would swing his arms like a cricket bat whenever he was thinking hard.

At the moment, he was deep in debate with this other man, and his head shook vigorously at regular intervals, his mane of hair shaking with the wind as he did so, giving him the look of a dog shaking water out of its fur. Altaf ran over and stood beside him, earning him a lovingly sharp clap on the shoulder from his father's chubby palm. I followed.

'Now, look here, Bhasharat, you told me the horse would be top-notch.'

'Arre yaar, how can the horse be any good if the owner takes no care of it?'

'I took the same care you did! And yet, you see, he collapsed as I was taking the tonga over Amira Kadal.'

'Ah, now if you overload the horse I cannot be answerable. Of course the poor horse cannot go over the slope of that bridge if you put fifty fat people in the tonga.'

'Come on now, Bhasharat!'

He shook his head once more.

'No. Price will remain same. No discount. And you are still a hundred and fifty rupees short.'

The man grimaced.

'Okay . . . now . . . I go back to old city. Think over it, Bhasharat. If you change your mind you let me know. Allah accepts repentance.'

Bhasharat Uncle rolled his eyes. The man turned and walked away, his back sloped and his knees turned outwards, so that he looked like a discouraged jungle cat, slinking away in the night.

'So!' Bhasharat Uncle barked, turning towards us, 'You've come for a ride, Zoon?'

'Yes, Uncle. I haven't been in a while.'

'No, you haven't! Good thing you've come. But did you see that man? Trying to cheat me out of a good horse. No, that *tongewala* was never an honest dealer. Pity my business needs the likes of him . . .' His grumbling faded away, vanishing almost completely, and he snapped back to the conversation at hand. 'So you two have fun! I'll be back at the house; your mother needs me for something,' he said, before trotting off down the path we'd come from.

'All right. Would you like to pick first?'

It took me a moment to register that Altaf was speaking to me, I was so deep in a maze of abstract thought. When it did, I let out an 'Oh!' of surprise and turned quickly to hide my embarrassment by trying to select a horse. I looked for the horse I'd seen many times before and always admired. I finally found him three stables from the left, below a battered sign bearing his name—Khurraam. He was all black, but not a shiny, deep black like night. He was a dull, light black, like burnt charcoal exposed to daylight for too long. His legs were thin and constantly knocking against each other. His tail was a misty grey, though Altaf maintained that it had not always been so. And his eyes were large and brown. I immediately chose him, not because he was beautiful, but because it didn't matter to him that he was ugly, because it didn't matter to him that he was old, because he never once considered that he might be better or worse than anyone else. He never gave more than what was expected; he never expected himself to give more than he gave. To me, somehow, he was beautiful.

I brought him out of the stable and thanked Altaf as he came over to help. I mounted him so swiftly and efficiently that I was slightly winded for a moment; I gripped at the frayed reins. Altaf walked over to his own horse, a deep brown thing with patches of white—Bijli.

He explained that they had recently got her from a man who seemed quite eager to be rid of her. Bhasharat Uncle was at a loss as to why she'd come so cheap, given that she seemed a fine specimen, healthy and strong. Uncharacteristically suspicious, he decided it'd do them best to hold off on presenting her to any buyers, lest his reputation suffer. This suited Altaf just fine as he was free to take her out whenever he liked; he had grown very fond of her.

She was a gentle horse, her eyes twinkling with the seeds of wisdom, never showing off, but always happy to be out on the fields. Altaf told me that he made a point of taking her out at least once a day. He maintained that she was the most energetic of the lot and didn't like being cooped up in a stable, but I suspected it was partly because he didn't like being cooped up in a stable himself.

'Now, we can't go far—the weather is pretty nasty today.'
'Yeah, I know.'

We moved slowly, the sun's rays shimmering down on us, pushing us forward. With the silence allowing my mind to dwell on that which I'd been trying to push away, I spoke little, and Altaf did not speak at all. My eyes remained glued to a spot on Khurraam's thin, untidy mane as his strained muscles rippled beneath his thick, black skin and the occasional drop of rain smacked against his back like a tiny bullet that shattered into millions of shards upon contact. My brow was furrowed with concentration, or anger, or worry, or sometimes all three at once.

We continued down the side of a near-hidden path, teeth chattering at the wind, soft voices at an enthralling sight, the persistent clicking of hooves on stone.

A conversation began, gradually at first, cautiously, like moving through a nursery at naptime, then slowly steadier, louder, until it began to flow like a chattering river.

'Your dad's business seems to be going well!'

'Oh, yeah, he's pleased with the demand for horses right now.'

'And you have an . . . older brother, right?'

'Yeah, Ma dotes on him. He's a cricket star. Dad keeps gushing about how he's made the team. He might even move to Mumbai or Delhi for further studies. And then there's me, kicking up leaves in the corner, doodling, collecting random stuff!'

I smiled to myself. Despite his clear reverence, I knew whose life sounded more interesting to me.

'He even gets the comfier bed. Cause of all his "physical exercise". *And* it's near the window. You know, when he came home with Dad last night, she made amazing haak.

And oh, the dum aloo! You should have seen it. The spices were so perfect, especially the cardamom. I, of course, was given something like a spoonful.'

I snorted with laughter. Just then, as though we'd remained content too long, Bijli neighed loudly and leapt up in the air. I gave a short cry; he'd barely managed to hold on.

She was so agitated that she continued to stamp her hooves and snort loudly until Khurraam, too, began to whinny nervously.

'What is it?' Altaf murmured, patting her thick neck.

We looked towards the house we were passing. It was an odd sort, almost eerie. Each window threw out a light that was dim and faded, like the rotting yellow of an ageing dress. The bricks were utterly black and chipped, and hung at random angles from the walls. The chimney stood far too rigid, like someone had fixed it in place with chains. I was just about to shake my head and tell myself sternly to not go about making up fairy tales when I felt a horrifying chill, as if an icy hand had gripped my, thumping heart in frost.

I gasped.

Altaf turned to give me a worried look.

I gestured that we should continue.

The moment we were at a fair distance from the house, the knot in my stomach began to ease.

'Who's house *was* that?' I panted, not really expecting an answer.

'Mus . . . Musta . . . Mustafa K. Bhukhari.'

I blinked slowly.

'What?'

'I read it on his mailbox. Mind you, it didn't look like it had been used for years, so it may just have been an old mailbox, but . . .'

I didn't—couldn't—respond.

'She won't be back soon, will she?' hissed the fireplace.

'No, I saw her running towards Altaf's house. She's probably stayed to eat or something,' responded the chair.

'Back to the topic, guys. What are we to do? She still thinks everyone can hear us. She has no idea of her true heritage. And I'm almost sure she suspects the chinar is beginning to decay,' said the desk.

'You don't know she's the only one,' put in the chair. 'I've always thought that Tathi—'

'It doesn't matter. She's not to know she's the only one who can hear us. She's not to find out about her heritage,' the fireplace spat out harshly, fighting against a wheeze.

The quill's speared tip abruptly pierced the heavy silence.

'You three. Always yapping. Ignoring the obvious.'

The fireplace was normally patient with the quill, whose eccentric ideas drove the desk to the edge, but then he felt tested, tired and utterly spent for understanding. 'Do tell us, dear quill,' he remarked, smirking. 'Perhaps we've forgotten to mark the date of the world's transformation into ice cream? Or have we lost that recipe for strawberry lemonade you gave us yesterday? Or could it even be that the queen of the Himalayas has lost her priceless shoe in the snow, as you'd begged us to consider the day before?'

'It is none of those things,' the quill responded, 'though they are all equally important. Thank you for reminding me to check that date, by the way. No, what I was going to say is that you are all ignoring the reason we're having this conversation at all—it's getting stronger.'

The air thickened.

'We've no proof at all that . . .' the chair trailed off.

'Yes we do. And we will continue to see more proof unless something is done about it.'

The fireplace's embers glinted a threatening red. 'It is meaningless!' he roared. 'Just because its power seems to be surging at the moment doesn't mean it isn't just . . . well . . . fluctuating, as it has done before.'

'Has it?' whispered the desk.

'Look here, nearly fifteen years ago, at this same spot, before me on this very carpet, every member of this house made a vow. A vow that Zoon would never be forced to become what her father did. A vow that we would keep our tragic past buried. I intend to keep that vow.'

'But at what cost?' the quill interrupted.

And silence began to smother them once more.

'Are you sure you're okay?' asked Altaf again as we began directing our horses home. 'You seem really shaken.'

I looked up from the patch of twisted, faded brown in a clump of fresh grass, running my tongue over the side of my mouth and finding it sore from my incessant gnawing.

'Oh, yes, I'm fine. It was just . . . that man whose house we passed . . . I know him.'

'You know, come to think of it, so do I!' Altaf put in. He pushed his, scraggy hair away from his squinting eyes so that it became even messier, and resembled something akin to a toddler's doodle on a tissue. 'He's a politician, right? I read something about him in the newspaper yesterday. Well, *I* didn't really read it, my dad told me about him; he reads the paper, like, first thing in the morning, even before the rest of us wake up! I've always thought it a bit odd. I mean, the news is always so depressing; wouldn't you rather sleep? But anyway, I . . .'

I looked up at the sky as Altaf rattled on. It was all thundering grey, with a few breaks of yellow light: a soft, fluffy handmade quilt torn by a careless child. I took a deep breath. The cool air felt calming yet sharp inside my heated chest.

'No, Altaf, I mean I know him . . . better than that.'

He paused, and then tilted his head questioningly, like a curious sandpiper lost at the brink of the shore.

Not even Ganapati, remover of obstacles, could ever understand the effort it cost me to speak my next words, to say out loud the very thing that I was dreading most.

'He's going to buy my house.'

'What?' Altaf looked flabbergasted, as I had been, yet he was responding differently. He stiffened, surprised, and his smile slipped to the muck, where it was crushed by a horse's hoof.

'Yes, the house is to be . . .' I couldn't bring myself to repeat it.

'No. It can't be. You're joking!'

His smile was attempting to fight the sudden shock, then to negate it, then to settle on pretending it hadn't happened at all.

But it had.

I shook my head and swallowed, trying to push past the lump in my throat that had swelled like a clot of blood as I spoke.

'But . . . but . . . where would you go?'

'I don't know. The city, Ma says.'

'This is the city!'

A bit surprised at the vehemence of his reaction, I took a minute to find the right words.

'I think she means . . . another city, Altaf. Maybe a bigger one. I think she means we'd try to leave Srinagar.'

I turned away. His voice, uncertain yet steady, hacked through the haze again. 'And you . . . you're okay with this? You don't seem to me to be the kind of person who just rolls over and accepts things. Not you!' he continued. 'Surely you're trying to stop this?' A dozen spines erupted beneath my skin, instantly placing me on the defensive.

'Of course I am, Altaf, but I'm just one—'

'Then maybe I can help!'

For the first time in all that my memories have preserved, I had been rendered utterly speechless. Altaf stared back at me like a determined little chipmunk on his first day of being enlisted to store nuts for the winter. His chin jutted out, an imperfect protrusion. It pushed out his lower lip, making him appear on the verge of throwing a tantrum.

I nearly snorted out loud. He was a bit ditzy, impulsive, distracted, maddeningly casual, and, to put it concisely, certainly not the type I'd have chosen as an accomplice. I was about to tell him exactly that (in a polite sort of way) when I stopped to rethink the obvious.

Of course, he was not the ideal ally, but it wasn't like I had a lot of options. Besides, his mother was good friends with mine, and might even prove to be an imperative tool in changing her mind. Moreover, he *did* live just down the street, so he'd be easily reachable if I needed him. Wait . . . would he?

I peered at him so long that he must have thought I needed glasses. Finally, I spoke.

'Well . . .' I began, still contemplating the matter, 'Well, do you agree that this—and this *only*—will be your top priority till we've prevented the sale?'

'I do!'

'Will you consistently and unfailingly be available for service?'

'I will!'

'And do you, Altaf, pledge yourself to this . . . mission, let's say . . . so as to in no way damage or discredit our aims?'

He nodded vigorously, and puffed out his chest, as though expecting to receive a badge of his membership to this honourable cause. I could never have said why, but at that moment, despite how little I yet knew of his life and his loves and his hopes, it seemed to me that we'd known each other for years.

'Then, Altaf Ali, I declare you part of the team!'

'YES!' he exclaimed, thrusting his fist in the air, startling poor Bijli for the second time. 'You won't regret it! This is, like, my first adventure! Let's do this!'

I allowed myself a small smile.

Once we'd ensured that our horses were safely back in their dilapidated stables and that Altaf had given them a large clump of hay that we knew wasn't enough, we walked back down the same path we'd taken. Halfway through a rather entertaining story about his cousin, his brother and a basket of strawberries, he gasped and began to jog quickly.

'What is it?' I asked, running after him.

'Oh, I was just talking about my brother and I remembered I'd promised to be home early so we could play cricket! We've got to finish before curfew. Even though he always beats me anyway.'

I rolled my eyes—how could anyone hurry so for a sport?—but kept up with him all the same. Seeing my raised eyebrows, he put in, 'I know you don't think it means much, but it's really special today. My father's just bought a new walking stick, so we've a new bat—we can use his old one now! We haven't had a new bat in years!'

I made an effort to look happy for him, which, surprisingly, wasn't too difficult. I could at least understand the joy that came with getting something new—such a rarity for us here.

We'd reached the front of his house, and I waved goodbye. The weight in my stomach had lessened since the morning, and I felt oddly light.

Just as he turned to walk inside, I called after him, 'Altaf! I need to ask you something!'

He stopped, with a single scraped foot on the creaky front step, waiting.

'Why does it matter so much to you if my house is sold?' Ma's decision had had such an impact on me that I hadn't even questioned Altaf's reaction. But why *should* he be so put out? It wasn't even his house!

'You're my friend, aren't you?' he responded. 'You know how hard it is for me to find friends? I'm not exactly in the position to pass up any at the moment. I can't have you just up and leave; I've only just met you! I mean, with you included, my total count of friends comes up to about . . . two. And the first one's my brother.'

With a final cheery wave, he swung open the front door, his fingers dodging the splinters out of habit.

I bit my lip.

There was that smile again.

Chapter Six

The chana man had fallen asleep, leaning tiredly against the post of his stand in the sun's gentle gaze. I waved at him anyway, wondering what he was dreaming of; perhaps of when his son would grow up, so he'd have some company in his stall . . .

The path home seemed unusually short that day.

The chinar tree seemed to leap out at me in desperation when I reached the creaky gate. My mouth fell open of its own accord. It was looking rather the worse for wear. Its leaves, a faded, sick shade of green, were droopy, and some were interspaced with holes. Its roots were jutting out of the ground, fighting to be released. I walked right over and hugged its massive trunk, as I used to when I was younger. It felt rough and scratchy, like jute, beneath my fingers.

'Hang in there,' I muttered. 'I promise I'll figure out what illness you've caught . . . I'll fix it, I'll set it right, *promise*.'

My first thought was of the fireplace. He was the oldest member of the house; surely he'd know what had happened to the chinar and how to set it right! Buoyed up by this thought, I let go of the tree.

The front door slammed with unnecessary force the moment I entered, as though admonishing me for being out too late. I hadn't. I'm not the sort to be irresponsible with time. I'm never out after dark, just like everyone else.

I could hear Ma's swift chatter from the living room. Despite a growing drowsiness, I was impressed—that telephone hadn't worked in years. It still kept cutting off, and occasionally I heard her honey-coated tones abruptly warp to some sort of snarl before immediately switching back the moment the phone began to work. I'd surely have to wait till she was done to speak to the fireplace. With no desire to know whom she was talking to or what they were talking about, I dragged my grating, bone-tired feet upstairs.

Just before I reached the top of the stairs, I froze, suddenly tense. I had heard a hurried, frantic whisper, in the same croaky voice that I'd heard before. I stood still, listening hard. The whisper echoed softly, as though caught within an endless tunnel. It seemed to be coming from my right; I turned and stared straight into solid wall.

I heard it again, coming from directly in front of me then. The voice was strained and panicked, yet so quiet I could barely make out that it was fighting to form words.

I knocked at the wood to see if it sounded hollow. But the beats of my knuckles were steady and firm, and no one spoke again.

Finally, I was forced to try and convince myself, as I had before, that I was just imagining things as a result of all this stress.

Collapsing on the bed seemed like an excellent idea, but I'd just realized that my feet had turned a shade darker, caked in a repulsive layer of filth that I couldn't escape. Looking in the mirror, I saw a few flecks of dirt sprinkled across my face like a dessert topping. I trod down the short hallway to reach the library. Tripping over a book thrown down against the carpet, I stumbled into the warmth of the armchair.

Before my skin even touched his smooth leather I sensed the tension oozing off him.

'So, how'd it go? Was it fun at Altaf's?' he asked, too quickly.

'It was fine, but . . . but . . . look—are you okay? You seem . . . I don't know . . . wait a minute . . . how did you know that I was at Altaf's?'

He fell silent, then tripped over words in his haste to respond, a juggler at the market who'd come dangerously close to dropping a prized egg.

'Well, we saw you. Through the window.'

'You're not even near the window. And I'm sure none of the books would have told you.'

'Of course, but . . . the . . . um . . . the desk and chair saw you. From downstairs. Of course, they argued for a while about whether it was really you or your long-lost twin, but—'

'So how did you get to know?'

Abruptly, he seemed to lose some of his nervousness in favour of squinting at me like I had just displayed the most supreme form of idiocy since Ma dusted down the whole house on a Sunday, before realizing it was Monday and she had to be at work.

'We're all one house, aren't we, Zoons? You think just because the fireplace and I are in different rooms I can't hear everything he's saying? Even though I may not . . . necessarily . . . agree with what he's saying . . .'

I peered at him.

'Anyhow, how was it at Altaf's? He seems nice. A bit off sometimes, but nice.'

I leaned backwards, exhausted.

'Oh, it was fine, you know, it—'

With a crash like a frying pan clattering against a bumpy floor, I flopped to the ground.

'Hai! Zoons! You okay?'

The books, who had been disrupted from their nap by my fall, began to chime in like an off-key choir, beginning with my grandfather's handwritten book of Kashmiri fairy tales.

'Of course she's not okay! Probably got a concussion! Police! Doctor! We need help!'

'Can we all just take a moment to review the facts of the case?'

'Anyone got some type of nut? We need to get some food into her.'

'No, no, what she needs is a good laugh. Provided by me. Humour is medicine. But there's nothing humorous about medicine! Ha, am I right?'

'Tut, tut. Look at her. This is a learning experience for all of you—she fell all wrong. If you fall, you must—'

'Can you stop acting like a first-aid manual? Just because you're the only sports magazine here . . . acting like you aren't YEARS old and deserve to be serving as some lady's tablecloth . . .'

'Now, look here, if you think that being Shanti's favourite romance novel means that you can be rude to everyone else—'

'I don't *think* it, darling. I *know* it.'

'All of you monkeys be quiet!' burst out the armchair, as usual.

I would have cut in earlier, perhaps rapped my knuckles on the bookshelves as I normally do, but I had been distracted by a curious glint, appearing as sunlight off water, coming from behind the last bookshelf. Whatever it was, it had been tucked away carefully, hidden yet not crumpled, nor hurriedly thrown, like an only child born out of wedlock. It was as though I had fallen into precisely the space needed to see it from; its placement was such that I doubted you could see it from anywhere besides directly behind and below the armchair.

I moved closer, tuning out the armchair's chastisements, the books' complaining and clamouring voices, and the insistent clatter of the bookshelves.

I crawled forward, as I've often seen people do when moving into the line of gunfire. Reaching forward, my fingers brushed against the fabric. Incredible! It was so soft it felt as though it had been made of clouds, for royalty . . . or for those in a happier place than this.

I stretched out further, gripped the jutting-out corner tightly and tugged so sharply that the armchair gasped. I turned. I hadn't realized he'd been watching me. It was then that I looked up and saw that the entire library was fixated on my actions. It was so quiet that you could nearly hear the sobs and sighs of our next-door neighbours.

I returned to my attempts to yank out the cloth, all the more focused then. There is something about having people watch you; the more people there are, the more ways you find to fail, no matter how simple the task.

With a final tug, it came tumbling out of the bookshelf, allowing the books near it to thud sharply against the hole it left behind. It shone brightly in my hands, despite being the deepest of blacks. Holding the rolled-up cloth under my arm, I pulled myself out of the crevice and back on to the armchair. My elbow was throbbing mildly from the fall, but I was too intrigued to care.

I rolled it out on the floor, pushing against the large bundle, then stepped back . . . and gasped. The entire thing had begun unfolding itself, as though it had been lying dormant, waiting, for years. I envisioned a criss-cross of unused, rusty railway tracks brought back to life. There were odd, sharp slaps when the ends of the cloth fell against the floor. I almost felt like I could hear the clicking and whirring of tiny gears within the cloth. Finally it seemed like it was finished. It was laid out before me in the grandest of fashions, almost as large as the library floor itself.

Upon it was a spidery network of silver and gold, and within it, myriad sharply stitched portraits. The cloth seemed to ripple against the ground, a darkened sea, and the portraits, a school of powerful fish.

'It's a . . . painting?' I whispered to myself, at a complete loss for any comprehension.

'It is a tapestry,' said the armchair, his tone heavy and serious, as though the inevitable had finally happened. 'A tapestry that tells of your family tree.'

In large, golden, sprawling letters, my last name—Razdan—was embroidered on the fabric. I knelt down, bending closer. Just beneath the family name, at the very top of the tapestry, there was a portrait of an aged man, seemingly a Pandit, his white hair a single tangled tuft. From him erupted four golden web-like lines moving downward, connecting him to four other portraits—three young men and a young lady—all staring up at me, unsmiling, the ghosts of the past lurking in their eyes. A silver strand on her side connected the young lady with a young man whose bushy eyebrows and hooked nose marked him as separate from their bloodline, yet whose place upon the tapestry marked him as part of the family.

My eyes began to race over the cloth, skittering over generations, over hundreds of years, before they were glued in place by a single portrait. There, shining up at me, stood Tathi, young and strong. No one had embellished the tales of her beauty. Around her, there were shifting beams of golden light, as though she was the sun of the portrait. Beneath her, I could make out a faded word scratched so lightly that one could tell that, unlike the others, this was not meant to last forever.

Rakshak

And from her ran a single golden link to—my heart skipped—my father. Tathi was not wrong; his nose was shaped exactly like mine. His hair was dark as Tathi's had been, his eyes wide-set and his mouth thin. It pained me that his portrait, like all the rest, was missing a smile. He looked up, unseeing and invisible; here, strong and whole, in reality, ravaged to charred flesh and ash by the heart of the devouring flame.

I wiped away the tear that had fallen against his face. My eyes skipped across to the portrait of my mother, connected to him by a bold line of silver, and then widened at the sight of her smile.

Hope surged in my heavy heart at the idea that hers, my mother's, was the only smile upon this tapestry. But then my spirits sank again. How did it matter if her portrait was smiling? She hardly smiled any more.

And there, growing from the two of them, like some sort of revolting tapeworm, was me. It was strange, how unfamiliar I looked.

I started. Around me, growing every second, was a beam of sunlight. Beneath me was a blurred word, becoming clearer by the moment. The light, like liquid gold, was slipping towards me from Tathi.

My heart had begun to race, so that it became impossible to tell one beat from the next, all thrumming together as a frantic ringing in my chest. My palms were so sweaty I could barely hold the tapestry.

I stood up, shaking. When I spoke, my voice came out rough and hoarse, whittled down by recent events to near nothingness. 'What is this?' I called out, my voice unusually shrill. 'What does it mean?'

The library was, for once, quiet.

Such was the silence that the fluttering of a few stray pages seemed magnified in the room. The books shuffled about, avoiding my gaze.

'Someone,' I said again. 'Someone explain this.'

One of the bookshelves coughed.

My patience, melting like the last layer of ice in summer, began to thin dangerously.

I turned towards the armchair, fuming at his sudden lack of support.

'Tell me. What have you been hiding from me all this time? Why didn't I know about this?'

Still he remained mute.

'Did anyone know about this at all?'

His silence, finally, infuriated me.

'If you don't tell me . . . I will leave this house today.'

They gasped. I would do nothing of the sort, of course, but that sort of anger is not easily overcome; it takes over your decisions. I sucked in a deep breath and felt my voice grow louder.

'I will call the realtor. I will allow Ma to sign the papers. We'll leave here right now.'

'Calm down,' came the voice of the armchair. At this moment, his steady, fatherly voice was fuel to the destructive flames of my fury. How dare he patronize me, sitting there and speaking to me as though I was in the wrong, as though my outburst was nothing but a tantrum? He had known this, he had known what it meant, and he hadn't bothered to tell me for fifteen years. I nearly shouted at him. But then again, I needed him to speak. So I held myself back as much as I could bear.

'Fine,' I spat out, forcing my tongue to move. 'Tell me. Now.'

The armchair sighed then, all of him inflating and deflating as he did. A voice echoed from the living room, so firm and bold that at first I did not recognize it as the fireplace's.

'Just tell her. We couldn't have kept it from her forever. We were stupid to try. She's old enough now; she's almost fifteen. We can't put this off any longer, armchair,' he said, bellowing through the wood as I'd never known him to.

'Is he crazy?' I hissed, and found myself whispering. '*This* is your method of communication? Ma will be up here any minute! Why is he being so lou . . .' My voice grew weaker, sapped by entirely unwelcome revelations. 'She can't hear any of you, can she? Not even when you're screaming? Not even when you move? I'm the only one who even knows there's something different about this house, aren't I?'

The armchair seemed to hesitate, weighing his response against absolute truth. When he spoke, he spoke so deliberately that he sent my mind into overdrive; I was trying desperately to find meaning in each word he uttered.

'Yes—you are . . . as far as we know.'

'*What?* Why didn't you just tell me?'

'You discovering and questioning this crucial oddity could have been your key to uncovering a terribly twisted past—one we never wanted to reveal to you! But I'm telling you now.'

I nodded slowly.

'Zoon, she cannot hear us because she is not from your bloodline.'

'She's my mother!'

'True. But she is not a descendant of the Kashmiri Pandit who first created this house, so long ago, in the hidden valley of Kashmir. He was the one who gave us our magic. He was the one who first realized what was causing misery in Kashmir, and how to stop it.'

'And what was it?'

I was not, for once, entirely sure I wanted to hear the answer.

'Kruhen Chay. The darkness.'

I shivered. The room seemed to grow colder and smaller as the armchair spoke.

'He is the cause of desolation in every country, in every human. And he had rooted in the once happy land of Kashmir. He is made up of our grief, of our suffering. It defines him. And he can kill viciously. He need simply engulf any human, consuming them, and it saps the magic and life right out of their blood, making him more powerful.'

He paused but then, as though already knowing this could in no way lessen the horror, went on.

'We cannot see him without a fire.'

'Does he fear it?'

'No. Not the flames themselves, not any more. But in his greatest form, he becomes visible in the smoke. And, more importantly, he is trapped by steam.'

'How?' I croaked hoarsely.

'It is water, Zoon,' the armchair replied gently. 'Being the diabolical, manipulative creature he is, he cannot come in contact with so pure a substance without it causing him harm. Have you never wondered why water is the most prominent element of any ritual in worship? Water dissolves shadow; water combats his parching, torrid form. And when water becomes steam, it has the power to engulf him, capture him and weaken him as nothing else can.'

He took a deep breath before continuing.

'The learned Pandit, your ancestor, was the first to realize this. He battled the darkness for years, seeking him out where he was strongest, forcing him back with water and flame, using ancient magic to diminish his pulverizing strength. The Pandit mapped out his weaknesses—steam, scriptures, confined spaces that restrained his slippery movement—and used the teachings passed down seasons of sun and rivers and wind to unearth chinks in his dark armour. He finally succeeded in trapping him in a cave, deep within the recesses of the earth. He created a room above that cave, a room that was filled with, and would, he hoped, always produce steam.'

'So . . . he's gone? He's not near here any more?'

'Zoon, listen. Panditji trapped him within that hollow and surrounded it with steam, but he knew that wasn't enough. So he built a house on top of it, and he poured all his magic into the house, and there he kept the darkness for hundreds of years.'

'And that house . . .'

He did not reply.

I was shaken. So Kruhen Chay was beneath us as we spoke.

'However,' he continued, 'the owners of the house were not careful enough.'

My heart skipped a beat, barely managed to catch the second, and thumped too loudly on the third.

'He escaped?' I whispered, in such hushed tones that I doubted the armchair had heard me. But he had.

He nodded gravely. 'The darkness was let out from the hammam. And in 1752, the Afghans began the rule of tyranny and oppression against the Pandits. They were taunted, abused, beaten, drowned . . . the seeds of misery began to swell within Kashmiri soil. The darkness regained his shape, and some sort of sustainable lifeline. Muslims weren't safe either . . . those that stood by the Hindus were deemed equally guilty. Families were torn apart. Religion became law. And their children, once pink-cheeked and bright-eyed, were dragged into a whirlpool of bitterness and blanketing rage, fuelled by humiliation and death. By around 1857, he was as powerful as he had been before he was imprisoned. And in 1931, he had enough control over Kashmir to inflict pain more acutely and fiercely. His hold on the people was almost unbreakable. A mob of Muslims . . . well, let me just say that it's astonishing what he can do to people when he's aided by helplessness and hunger.'

'They attacked the Hindus?'

I was so horrified I couldn't speak louder than a frantic hush.

'Yes. It was a movement against the oppressive Maharaja. Buildings and bodies alike were burnt and ravaged. The darkness fed off their suffering, and it gave Kruhen Chay a gush of power and strength. Debates were held, resolutions passed, but he rendered all worthless. By 1947, the revolts had begun. He grew stronger by the day, until finally his power rose to an absolute height.'

'The raids,' I murmured.

'Indeed. There was nothing anyone could do. He was everywhere—in the saturated, heavy clouds that blanketed us in his wrath, in the unseen cobwebs within our homes and minds, latching on to despair, in our hearts, swelling like a tick at the slightest emotion—so that the people turned into the walking dead, a rotted soul inside a barely moving body. We could no longer see the light of the sun. We could no longer feel the cool of the rain. It was not so much Kashmir as what was left of it. We distrusted each other. Men who had never met became enemies. Families that had been interlinked for generations hacked away their bonds as if they were weeds. And in the winter of 1947, after the Partition, the climactic bloodshed began. The fireplace had told me once, when I was brave enough to ask, that it was something out of a psychopath's nightmare; that people would shoot at the body before they discerned a face; that flames of the dead, or dying, would cough out black steam into the sky; that you would walk on the whispering streets at night and wince at a crunch beneath your feet, not knowing whether it was a tree branch or a human arm . . . And that madness seeped through the streets like a noxious contagion, poisoning the minds and hearts of the once gentle people. The echoing sound of murder burst through the filthy lanes: the crack of a neck, the gurgle of water-corrupted lungs, the shredded cries of those lost to the flames, the wretched screams of those not lucky enough to be murdered outright. They were terrifying times. Hindus were tortured, pillaged, abused, forced to convert, and flung out of their homeland, normally not all in one piece. Muslims were left bitter, weak and miserable. The people of Kashmir began drowning in deranged militancy. They lost any identity and, with their identity, their hope for the future.'

'What did we do?' I asked. Because we had to have done something. We couldn't have remained dull and unmoving. We just *couldn't* have.

'Yes, the house did do something,' the armchair said, reassuring me after sensing my desperation. 'The darkness's power erupted as the genocide did. But the growth of his power only led to a growth of ours. The peak of his power prompted the house to create a Guardian. And the first Guardian was him.'

The armchair gestured to a portrait towards the left of the tapestry. I leaned down towards it.

His name was Rahul Razdan, and his eyes seemed deeper than the rest, as though there was a whole world inside them. He was skinny and looked weak, yet there was something about him that evoked a sense of a hidden mass of power just beneath his pale skin.

'So the Guardian protects the house by . . . what, sitting on the doorstep with a stick or something?'

The armchair laughed, but the edges of his normally hearty laugh were frayed by a bite of bitterness.

'No, Zoon. The Guardian is much more than that. A Guardian may wear the magic of the house as a cloak upon his shoulders and a sword upon his hip, and he must guard it as jealously as a rakshasa guards his gold. And our Guardian must have a strong, large heart, to protect this realm of magic. The Guardian is, after all, a concentration of the magic of this house. Should the darkness attack, the Guardian must defend against it, using the enchantment passed down through generations, thus fending off the creature once more for another few decades of so-called peace.'

He paused abruptly, waiting to see if I was taking it all in.

'The creation of a Guardian was so impactful that for a while after the Partition, there was peace, blessed peace. The Indian Army arrived to restore order, and did, for the most part, succeed. But it was too good to last for longer than a few months. Since then, the darkness has been battling and breaking through your predecessors to get to, and sap the core of, Kashmir's happiness: this house. And may I say, he has not been entirely unsuccessful.'

I glanced once more at the tapestry, and my heart lurched. Few Guardians had lived beyond the age of thirty.

'But where did Kruhen Chay come from?'

'I don't know. No one does. I only wish I did. Very little is known about the darkness. Except that he may be . . . getting stronger.'

'I know,' I replied. It struck me then that I had always known. The violence, the loss of any liveliness, the militancy . . . it couldn't be more clear that Kruhen Chay was beginning to manifest himself within Kashmir once more. And yet another piece of the horrific, torturous puzzle clicked into place. It was not disease suffocating the chinar outside. I might have guessed it earlier, had I stopped a moment to think. It had never once shed its leaves in living memory. But then . . .

It couldn't *die,* could it?

I began to lose myself in my thoughts when a final question beckoned me back to reality.

'And my father?' I asked.

As always, my mind immediately conjured up a dozen gaudy distractions, my heart began to thump too quickly in an attempt to help me get away from my own body, and my limbs grew heavy and sedated, longing for sleep and misting over my thoughts.

I ploughed on. 'What happened to him? He didn't just die from suffocation, did he? There had to be something more than smoke that killed him?'

The armchair became still, like he was contemplating how exactly to untie a matted knot that had been left in place for years.

'Your father was . . . well, he was always very motivated to become the Guardian . . . but when motivation turns into something darker . . .'

'What went wrong? Tell me!' I spat out frantically.

'He was so convinced of his own strength, so convinced that it was his duty to be a better Guardian than all those before him, that he took the role when he'd barely turned thirteen.'

I gasped. How could he? Surely, *surely* it had been too much for him? And then it struck me—of course it had been too much for him. He was *gone,* wasn't he?

A dull lump of lead settled in my stomach. 'All right. Great story, armchair. Thanks,' I murmured, strangely miserable, which was odd, considering I didn't even remember what he looked like. People say it is not possible to wholly love someone you have never known. I say that it is only ever possible to wholly love someone you have never known, for once you have met them even for a short while, you will undoubtedly find something unlovable about them. Vaguely I recalled my shrill, shrieking screams at my mother.

'The *story*,' the armchair continued, then distinctly ruffled, 'wasn't *finished.* Now, I'm going to complete this story, and if you open your silly mouth once more, I will shove my springs up your bottom whenever you try to sit down.'

I snapped my lips shut and waited, smiling slightly. It was so rare to see the armchair out of sorts.

'So your father, as I was saying before I was so rudely interrupted, became Guardian at an unthinkably young age. He believed he would be the finest protector of the house since the Panditji himself. His deluded confidence made him sure that he could destroy Kruhen Chay entirely, without any need to battle or even trap it! The years went on, and his arrogance turned into bitterness and cruelty. Poor Shanti could not understand his sudden fits and rages.'

The armchair stammered over a few hurried words before sighing softly, as though he wanted to say more, but there was no more to say.

'So one day, when he felt the wind was moving in the right direction, he summoned the darkness to the hammam, underneath which the cave—where it had first been trapped—was hidden.'

'He *summoned* it?' I blurted out. 'He could do that?'

'Well, he gloated about his godlike power to all who would listen. He would seek out the darkest and most dangerous parts of Srinagar, and yell out brash and foolish challenges to the wind. He made it clear to Kruhen Chay that he wished to fight, so of course he wasn't kept waiting.'

The bitter edge to the armchair's voice came seeping like toxic gas through the cosy air of the library.

'Kruhen Chay destroyed him. When his body was found, he seemed to have been killed from the smoke; suffocation, they said. It was passed off as a freak accident.'

I felt as though a large lump of rotting food was being digested slowly and painstakingly. I could not speak.

'But,' I choked out, 'where is Kruhen Chay then? The Guardian was utterly defeated! Why isn't the house razed yet?'

The armchair responded with something akin to embarrassment. I wouldn't know exactly. I'd never seen him embarrassed before.

'We . . . don't . . . know.'

I was dumbstruck. They didn't know? How could they not know? They were the house! They saw it all happen!

'It must have been some kind of miracle that protected us. All we know is that the darkness was forcefully expelled. We believe it might have been the overflow of protective power—the counteraction from such complete annihilation of a Guardian. And we have not had a Guardian nor seemingly needed one for a while,' he finished.

'But you may need one now . . .'

The armchair didn't reply.

'But you know what?' I burst out. 'If the house is sold, we'll never be able to help anything anyway, so why don't we just focus on that?'

I flopped, exhausted, into the armchair.

'Sorry,' I continued, 'it's just that I feel like we're getting nowhere with stopping this stupid sale!'

'That's not true,' said the armchair loyally. 'We have made progress. We just need a bit more momentum to shut it down entirely.'

His encouragement made me feel a bit better. I thought of Altaf, our new recruit, and then of all that I had to tell him. My racing heart began, slowly, to calm. The heat in my muscles began to fade away.

'You know,' I said, creases forming along my forehead from thought, 'there's something I don't like about this Bhukhari. He's just not right, somehow . . . he creeps me out.'

'I absolutely agree,' said the armchair vehemently. 'He seemed terribly shifty to me from the moment he arrived. Why, of all the people in Srinagar, did he have to be the only one interested in the house?'

'He wasn't,' I responded. 'There were others, they were just . . . delayed . . . for various reasons . . . because . . .' I didn't finish my sentence. Suddenly, shrewd suspicion leapt up inside me. What had held those customers back? To what lengths would this politician go to buy—to *steal*—my house?

At once, the armchair let out a furious whisper, as if he could not have held himself back a second longer. 'Tell me,' he asked hurriedly, 'have you felt it?'

I was so startled by his sudden fervour that I did not answer. 'Have you felt your abilities begin to grow? Have you sensed your connection to the house becoming stronger? Have you been able to do things that you haven't been able to before?' he continued.

I thought hard, frantically collecting my jumbled thoughts to answer his question. But I could not formulate a satisfactory response, and I doubted that I'd even understood him properly. Do things with what? What sort of things?

A flash of the brightest white outside the window interrupted my thoughts. I raced over to the frosted glass and called out, 'It's snowing, everyone!' This was met with appreciative whoops, the occasional cheer and soft voices of congratulations from the older and more sophisticated volumes. Grinning, I pressed my nose against the glass. Outside, the world was beginning to be hidden beneath a swirling white, like someone had finally shaken up an antique snow globe. The trees donned elegant jackets of frost white, and the grass shone in the moonlight, sprinkled with crushed ice. The moon itself burst through the haze as the centre of it all, releasing sparkles of the purest silver upon the earth. Even from the library, I could hear the wind whistling through the thick, ancient chimney, the gentle sound of a Kashmiri hymn in the night.

I heard Ma's precise footsteps in the hallway, the sound of each step against the floor exactly the same as the last, a sharp, ringing slap. She swept in, her wiry hair and tired eyes displaying that she'd spent the evening cleaning. In her right hand she clutched the rag I'd spent the morning dirtying, and it didn't look any cleaner for having been dragged through the house. That twinge of guilt twisted my insides once more, but I pushed it away hurriedly, refusing to prod, provoke or explore it.

'Dear,' she began, and my heart sank instantly—her tone was icier than the freshly fallen snow. 'I wanted to let you know—the date of the sale has been moved to the day before your birthday. Mr Qureishi has said that the buyers will have been decided by then.'

I nodded distractedly, and then froze. 'Ma . . . my birthday's day after. The house will be sold . . . tomorrow?' The horror on my face must've been unmistakable.

'Well, y-es, yes it will.'

'Then why didn't you just say tomorrow? Were you trying to sugarcoat it for me? Because if so, that completely failed.'

Panic was rising inside me like a growing tide, and I could feel my brain thrashing against my skull like a furious, frothy white wave. If the house was to be sold tomorrow, we'd be out within a week! Just as I was about to erupt, I saw the notebook jumping wildly behind Ma's back. Words had been slashed across him, so poorly written that, at first, I squinted to make them out.

StAy 4 BiRthday

I stared. Then, with a jolt of understanding, I cried out, 'Ma! I have to ask you something!'

Surprised by my intensity, she took a moment to respond. 'Yes, Zoon?'

'I know that you really want to sell this house. And . . . I know that we shouldn't keep buyers waiting. But I wanted to ask you if we could please, please stay here for my birthday. It'll be my fifteenth birthday, Ma, and I want to spend it here with Tathi.'

'Genius move!' muttered one of the bookshelves.

Ma hesitated for what seemed like a decade, weighing each outcome against the other, against how much this might mean to me. Finally, she gave a tired sort of sigh, melting the chill out of her voice, and replied, 'Sure. You've been on your best behaviour, so I don't see why not. I'll let Mr Qureishi know he has to begin the selling and moving the day after your birthday instead, all right, Zoon?'

I glowed with the flush of success.

'Thank you so much, Ma!'

And I rushed forward to pull her into a tight hug.

'Oomph!' Ma huffed. Then she tapped me playfully on the head, saying, 'Silly girl. Oh, is it snowing already?'

I nodded into her shoulder.

'All right then, time for you to go out and get some dry wood off the lawn for the *bukhari*. I'll get the food ready.'

Bringing in the firewood was one of my favourite things about winter. Ma would set up the bukhari in the front room so that we could look out of the window. I'd rush out to grab as much firewood as I could in the crisp, pure snow until my cheeks were pink from the cold. Then I'd run back inside with the wood and Ma would be waiting with hot kehva. We'd toss the wood into the bukhari and then cook our food on top of it, before eating dinner huddled round the flames with a blanket and a pillow or two.

It had been that way for Ma when she was a child, and she'd insisted on passing on that experience to me, despite the fact that we had a working fireplace. The unbending tradition did not fail us today.

Outside, the world seemed crystallized in peace, something so rare here that I stopped and stared till my bare feet could no longer stand the cold. I rushed in quickly with the wood, and handed it over to Ma. Resting against the door for a moment, I saw the fireplace sulking in the other room. This *does* make him feel neglected. Despite all his wisdom, he can be quite childish sometimes.

Ma was already seated on a couple of pillows and, after stoking the fire, passed me some kehva. Grinning, I joined her, and lay flat on my belly against the fluffy carpet.

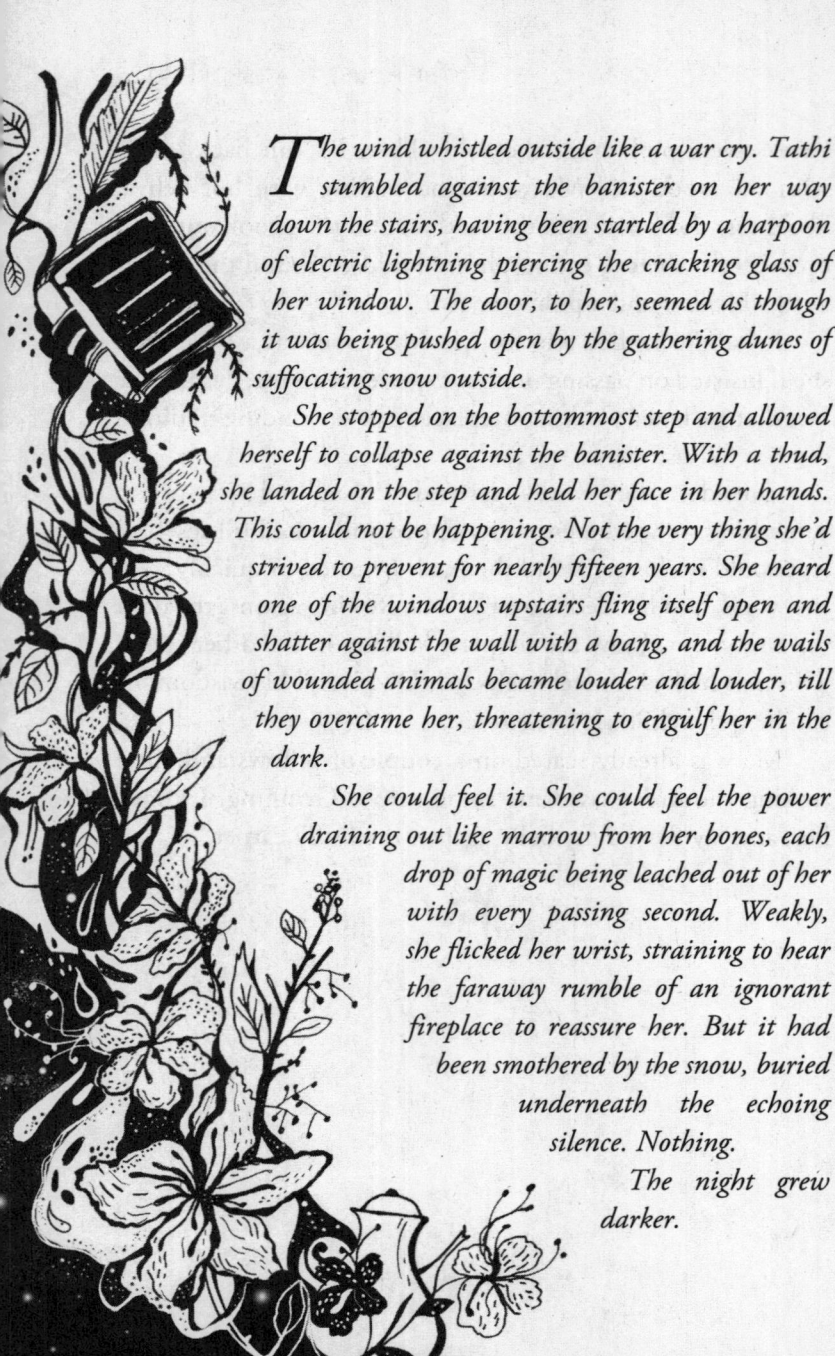

*T*he wind whistled outside like a war cry. Tathi stumbled against the banister on her way down the stairs, having been startled by a harpoon of electric lightning piercing the cracking glass of her window. The door, to her, seemed as though it was being pushed open by the gathering dunes of suffocating snow outside.

She stopped on the bottommost step and allowed herself to collapse against the banister. With a thud, she landed on the step and held her face in her hands. This could not be happening. Not the very thing she'd strived to prevent for nearly fifteen years. She heard one of the windows upstairs fling itself open and shatter against the wall with a bang, and the wails of wounded animals became louder and louder, till they overcame her, threatening to engulf her in the dark.

She could feel it. She could feel the power draining out like marrow from her bones, each drop of magic being leached out of her with every passing second. Weakly, she flicked her wrist, straining to hear the faraway rumble of an ignorant fireplace to reassure her. But it had been smothered by the snow, buried underneath the echoing silence. Nothing.

The night grew darker.

She dragged herself upstairs as if through barbed wire, and felt the familiar hole slash open wider inside her, her body aching for tears that she could no longer produce. No more than a tired old lady, she threw herself into bed and mourned her only son.

'My boy,' she murmured, paralysed where she lay, 'how I cared for you. How I warned you. How I care for them still. Oh, where have you gone? You abandoned me . . . I am lost. My child . . . when will I see you again? Ah, soon, I hope . . . I pray . . .'

And her voice faded into emptiness in the storm that was Kashmir.

Chapter Seven

I can normally never tell just by how a dream is going what is likely to happen when I wake up. I often mistakenly relate the way a dream unfolds to how I will feel once I wake. But that, of course, is hardly ever the case. For example, I could be trembling through a nightmare of the most terrifying, disgusting night-crawlers scuttling hidden beneath the floorboards, and then wake up to find Ma waiting with hot milk and a kiss. Or I could be dreaming of discovering a hidden island, filled with fantastical creatures, only to be woken, as I was today, by a horrible creaking noise that made nails on a chalkboard sound like the melodies of Tansen.

At first, I was almost sure I'd imagined it, for the bedroom seemed as rumpled and quiet as ever, the portraits silent but for the occasional snore or grunt. Then I heard it again—a sharp scraping noise that sounded like someone was twisting a robot's arm off. With a jerk, I catapulted out of bed. Hurriedly, I flung on a mishmash of creased clothing, brushed my hair just to the point where no one could mistake me for a homeless person and burst out of the bedroom door.

It was then that I caught the quiet gabble of voices coming from downstairs. I nearly groaned aloud.

Once I arrived downstairs, my worst fears were immediately confirmed. What was once a peaceful living room had been converted into a harbour of sweaty men who roamed around checking this and that, making notes on little scraps of paper and occasionally moving over to Mr Qureishi who, I noticed, had seated himself grandly in the front room on the chair like some emperor.

Both the desk and the chair were unusually grim and silent; they had, at last, found something they could agree on.

Ma was leaning nervously on the desk, twisting her thumbs together, her eyes darting from person to person. Whenever a man came over to talk gruffly about work to be done and further pay, she'd nod and mutter, while neither the man nor Mr Qureishi paid her any attention. I could have smacked my head against the wall just to end all of this, and the day had barely begun.

I walked over to them and gave Mr Qureishi a smile so tight and lifeless that it could hardly have been mistaken for anything other than a sign of wholehearted dislike.

'Ma,' I asked her, my lips still pressed together in a furious smile, 'what are these people doing here?'

'Well,' she responded, glad to finally have an opportunity to make her seem in charge, 'they've come to help us whip the house into shape. For the buyers.'

'So many of them?' I muttered, looking around at the flurry of movement; they looked like a flock of squawking geese as they moved from here to there, inspecting the kitchen range, knocking on the sturdy walls and sighing at the old wiring that I'd never known us to have any problems with. The sheer number did nothing to improve my mood. I dragged my feet across the carpet and into the living room, mainly to get away from Ma and the realtor, the two people who seemed to be successfully recruiting members and sponsors for the Make-Zoon-Miserable foundation.

I came across a man lying flat on his back in the bathroom, a toolbox open near his feet—evidently the source of the horrible creaking that had woken me. Before I could speak, I heard a sudden shriek and jumped at the noise, gasping.

The plumber turned fleetingly to stare at me with a look normally reserved for the unhinged. I stared steadfastly at my toes, trying hard not to look too excited, for I had recognized the call as belonging to the rusty, grated voice I'd been hearing in the walls.

'Zoon!' came the short cry once more.

The plumber gave a great sigh, rubbed his grimy, blackened hands on his equally filthy shirt and exited the bathroom with some difficulty, presumably to speak to Ma about a change in payment for his services—again. I slammed the door behind him; in the general chaos, it went unnoticed.

My head snapped around, ears pricked and eager to identify the speaker.

'Me! Down here!'

My gaze fluttered to the metal tube that had been in the plumber's hands. It hung half in and half out of the wall, seemingly stretching to come closer to me. I knelt down at once, bending low in case anyone else came by to question my sanity.

'That's it! It's excellent to see you at last, I must say . . . although I'd imagined you to be . . . bigger somehow . . .' began the pipe.

'You're the one I've been hearing inside the walls?' I muttered, astonished.

'Yes, of course. I'm one of the pipes. We've been trying to speak to you, Zoon, because it's of vital importance that you understand what I'm about to tell you.'

His hurried voice dropped an octave and became deep and silken as molten chocolate, so that I had to lean forward to catch his next hushed words.

'These pipes are imperative to you. Do you understand? We were built with the house itself. The majority of us do not carry water; we carry steam. We were not made to be simple plumbing. We are your protection.'

There was a faint ringing in my ears.

'The armchair told me . . . he said . . . steam is better than smoke because . . .'

'Yes, yes,' cut in the pipe, speaking quicker then. 'And that's why we could be your greatest asset in the looming battle, alongside your growing powers. When you need us—'

'Hold on! There's going to be a bat—'

'Don't interrupt, we haven't got time—that man will be back any minute to shove me back into the walls again. So listen to me. Call us, and we will come. Got it? We are a part of your army, as we have always been, and we will not hesitate to aid you valiantly on the battlefield. Magic and light *will* trump over evil. Never fear.'

'But—what—wait—'

He had rattled on so fast I had barely caught his words.

There was so much I wanted answered: what battle was he talking about? How did I fit into all of this? I couldn't fight battles! What did he mean I have powers? Unusual things had been happening, yes, but . . .

At that precise moment, I heard heavy stomps amidst the racket outside, and straightened up again. The plumber marched in once more, a tuft of green sticking out of his front pocket, brushing past me as though I'd been nothing more entertaining than a slug. He bent down where I'd been moments earlier, roughly ramming the poor pipe back into its alcove in the wall. I glared at the plumber, suddenly ensnared by a haughty dislike.

'Are you breaking our pipes?'

He looked up, and I noticed then that his face was crudely moulded, like putty by a child, his eyes an odd, misted grey, and his mouth so twisted that I could never tell whether he was smiling or grimacing. His lumpy cheeks were blanketed in rough grey stubble, enough to make him seem dishevelled but not enough for him to spend money on a shave. He stared at me a moment too long before responding, and already the atmosphere was uncomfortable.

'No, I'm just fixing them.'
'For whom?'
'The people in this house.'
'I'm the people in this house.'
'Yeah, but . . . the new people in this house.'
'There aren't any new people.'
'For you, then. I'm fixing them for you.'
'I don't want them fixed.'

'Look, kid, I've got to work on this. I can't play now, all right?'

'Don't break my pipes.'

The plumber sighed at the ceiling, spared me half a second's glance and then went back to twisting the bolts on our rusty pipes.

A weary irritation simmered inside me, weary because it had already been felt so many times before. I stared intensely at the bolt that the plumber was working on. It was a small bit of metal jutting out from under the sink, and it appeared to me like some sort of clawed foot creeping out from under the browning white. It pressed against the pipe around it, as though it had been jammed into an opening far too small. Upon closer inspection, it seemed to be shivering, like it was dying to escape. Sold. *Sold*. SOLD. The brash, angry thought grew wider and wider in my mind, till it had shoved out everything else, and all that was left was an awareness of my own misery and the image of that silly bolt.

Suddenly, the bolt popped out of its socket, as though launched from a slingshot. It smacked the plumber on his sagging right cheek, narrowly missing his eye. I started, and he cried out in pain and surprise.

I stood there like a wax statue, with my eyes wide and demented as he rubbed off the first layer of his skin while swearing furiously. My fingers fidgeted ceaselessly, scuttling around the back of my hands like insects, searching for a way out. The armchair's words, then pressed forth by the pipe's, stirred darkly in the back of my mind. I certainly had never been able to move bolts before. Not without having laid a finger on them anyway. And certainly not at *that* speed.

I took a deep, shaky breath. But I hadn't made that happen, I told myself. I *hadn't*.

Then, guiltily, I began to wonder . . . would it be so terrible if I had? What was wrong with using this new-found power to help stop the sale? I was saving the house, wasn't I?

A moment later, every bolt in the pipework burst out like fireworks, showering the plumber with sickeningly filthy water and leaving him spluttering out curses. Grumbling, he began all over again.

I shut the door to the bathroom with a slight smile.

Immediately, I felt my spirits rise further. From an open window in the front room, beyond the sounds of blades hacking through wallpaper and Ma's meaningless trills, I heard a voice that was light and excited trying to force itself into a serious and meaningful tone.

'I mean, really,' Altaf was saying, 'do you honestly think you could get good money for this dump? You wouldn't even fetch a fair price for the doorstep.'

'Do I *know* you?' responded Mr Qureishi coldly, his eyebrows raised and his body tilted resolutely in the other direction. His disgustingly large nose sniffed scornfully while Altaf ploughed on.

'See, if you really wanted to make big bucks, you'd go for the better houses, the ones with the huge TVs and fancy gates that I'm not allowed in. I mean, how can your work be fun if you don't even get paid properly?'

'Well, it isn't supposed to be a picnic! And I do quite enjoy it. I'm just not sorry to have to go home once it's over, all right?'

'I think maybe you should think about doing something else. How about a food stand? Everyone loves food. Yes, I think you should definitely open a small kebab corner down the road. How long have you been selling these dumb houses? How old are you anyway?'

'I'm forty-three!' responded Mr Qureishi, flushing angrily.

I'd stuffed my fist into my mouth to keep from bursting into laughter.

Altaf didn't seem to have bothered listening to his answer. 'What about your family? Aren't they important to you? Shouldn't you be spending time with them?'

'Of course they're important to me! I visit my aunt in Gulmarg every two weeks. Or . . . sometimes less if . . . you know, the bus fee gets high . . . or curfew doesn't allow me to . . .'

'What about your wife? Don't you love her?'

'I'm not married.'

'I'm sure your children would grow and blossom into beautiful young members of society, if only you spared some time for them as a loving father would.'

'I'm *not married.*'

'I mean, it's a Sunday, for the love of Allah. Shouldn't you be doing something fun?'

'Well . . . I wouldn't say no to some hot kehva . . . and a magazine, perhaps . . . my own garden is a great place to read, you know . . .'

'Yes, I fully agree, I like cooking too. Don't you just love that feeling of a warm, home-cooked meal with your kids?'

Mr Qureishi slammed his eyes shut, as though refusing to acknowledge his own frustration, muttering furiously about what pay he really ought to get for all the emotional lunatics he had to deal with.

I walked over, pretending to scratch my nose to hide my wide smile. But just as I crossed the doorstep, burying my foot up to my ankle in a puddle of melted snow, I heard Altaf speak again.

'But we're getting off topic. I think we should return to my original point; you've really nothing to gain from selling this house.'

'Nothing to gain? It's my job, you meddling boy! And for your kind information, the deal has been closed for more money than you've ever possibly dreamt of. We're selling to the most important politician in Kashmir! So you may now go and bother someone else, thank you very much.'

I didn't bother listening for Altaf's rebuttal. He may even have called out to me, but I could no longer pay him any attention. I felt as though a large dead animal had found its way into my stomach, and its rotting limbs were clogging up my airway. I spun straight around and marched back into the house. My eyes were caught by the chinar—leaning weakly against the straining wood, leaves all but lost in the tempest of life, those that were left curdling in decay . . . My vision blurred and dropped—bark growing parched and rough, sickly shades of ecru worming into the brown, a single crack trailing up its centre. My heart lurched to pull me closer, and yet I did not change course. I was sure that if I did, the forbidden tears burning the corners of my eyes would finally begin to leak through.

Catching Ma roughly by the arm, I spat, 'We're selling to *him*?'

'Goodness, Zu! You scared me!'

'We're selling to that horrid fellow?'

I couldn't understand my own mind. How could this have come as such a rude shock?

But it had. I swallowed hard.

'Don't be rude, Zoons. Mr Bhukhari is a perfectly respectable man. And yes, we are selling to him. I thought you knew that already.'

'You don't even want to . . . I don't know, just . . . consider some other buyers?'

I was grasping at straws. I knew that. So when she bit her lip and twisted up her dupatta in one fist, it wasn't the reaction I'd expected.

'Now . . . don't take this the wrong way, Zoons, but . . . he's offered far more than the set amount, so . . . so the deal has been closed.'

I was silent. Did she expect me to get angry? I wasn't angry. I just felt a dull, heavy weight inside me, like my heart was made of lead. Hopeless. It was all just hopeless. Behind her, from the living room, I saw the fireplace. A few embers were spluttering sharply beneath his logs, fighting to stay alight. Then one of them launched itself on to the foot of an electrician passing by, who hopped lightly, hissing at the pain.

Despite the numbness leaking out slowly from my frigid brain, I heard Mr Qureishi's abruptly squeaky voice come through the garden again.

'What is it going to take to get rid of you, boy? You and that whiny little brat of a girl! No wonder you're friends.'

'Now, just a minute!' Altaf spat back, anger beginning to brew dangerously beneath his words. 'Don't you talk about . . . don't speak like . . .'

I couldn't stay there a second longer. I knew I was meant to—my insides squirmed horribly at the thought of leaving my worries to the wind—but if I did, I would probably end up doing something impractical, like scream or sob.

'Ma, can I go out?' I burst out, thinking only of leaving as quickly and unnoticeably as I could. My voice was steadier than I'd expected it to be.

She turned back to me.

'Sure. Where to?'

'Oh, I don't know, I just . . . I feel like a walk. Is that okay?'

I wasn't lying. I wasn't even arguing. I felt like all the fight had been sucked out of me, and I slumped where I stood, a deflated balloon, rippled rubber lying heavily against my skin.

She stared at me, her eyes shining with concern. Then she pulled me forward into a quick, swift hug. It was so unexpected that I didn't have time to tailor my response to the precise needs of the situation, and I simply hugged her back. In all this time I'd spent trying to sabotage her plans, I'd forgotten how much I loved her. I'd forgotten how much I cared for her. I remembered then.

'Sure it's fine. Just take your umbrella. Mr Qureishi said it might rain.'

Mr Qureishi turned out to be entirely wrong, which made me feel a lot better. The sky was a dusty blue, and the clouds were suspended like wisps of used tissue in the air. The umbrella struck pointlessly against the rough, dry road. Every inch of the breathtaking snowfall had gone as quickly as it had come. Once I began nearing the city centre, I noticed that there was hardly anyone chattering at the storefronts, dragging along creaky wheelbarrows or haggling loudly and over each other only to finally settle on the original price. The whole place seemed oddly abandoned. I lifted up the umbrella and held it under my arm. The silence was thick as tar and lingering in the dampened air. Slowly, I crept to the side of the road and began to walk behind the houses and fences, an offender of disrupting peace avoiding detection.

I had hardly noticed where my feet were taking me, but I realized then that I was much further away from familiar territory than was normal. My pulse quickened beneath my sweaty skin. My back hunched over, as if trying to shield me from the invisible bullets striking me through unseen eyes. I spun about quickly and began to walk homeward. The Kashmir around me was still and unmoving. Not so much as a leaf had turned to bid me goodbye.

Just then, a glint, like that of a hidden rupee in a gutter, caught my eye. There, beyond a few broken-down, rickety fences, was a brash, oversized building with glass windows and a twisted, fancy door handle. I'd never seen anything so . . . big and . . . well organized. Not around here anyway! I stepped closer, still hidden by the pattern of shadows etched on to the faded pavement. There was a large doorman at the gate, his hands clasped in front of him and his nose tilted so high it was a wonder he could reach it with a handkerchief. His palms were larger than my face and he looked like someone had filled him up to the brim with air.

There must have been something encouraging in the breeze that day, because I walked right over to him without a second thought. Perhaps it was because I could see that he was and always had been a doorman, and not part of the military. Perhaps it was because I felt I could probably outrun his large, clearly clumsy feet. Perhaps it was even because his skin was precisely the same tanned brown as mine.

'Excuse me,' I piped up when I reached him, 'but who lives here?'

'It's not a house. It's an office,' he responded distastefully. Horrid manners.

'Whose office, please?'

'It's Mr Mustafa Bhukhari's office.'

'Oh! The politician?' I gasped. He stared at me, his left eye squinted, seeming to think I didn't warrant a reply.

'I . . . um . . . I need to see him. I mean, meet with him. Is he in?'

'Yeah, he's in. But he said he's not to be disturbed. My pay's depending on that and I need it. So buzz off.' Excitement shot up my spine, and my brain—tired and fed up until this moment—zipped about like a March hare to process this new information.

If I could just speak to Mr Bhukhari and convince him that he ought not to buy the house, request him even, maybe I could still salvage a solution from the day's horrible turn of events. The very thought of appealing to his better nature was,

I'll admit, repulsive, but I was desperate. The only question then was whether this thickheaded walrus would let me in.

'I'm sure he would make an exception for *me*,' I put in, a simpering smile stretching across my face.

The doorman peered at my too-innocent look.

'And who are you exactly?'

'I'm . . . um . . .'

'Identification?'

Uh-oh. Think quick, Zoon.

My fingers were on the brink of squirming, my voice had grown softer and my eyes were fighting the strong impulse to dart away from his suspicious gaze, desperate for an escape.

So you know what I did?

I drew myself up to my full height (even stood up on my toes to gain half an inch extra) and raised my eyebrows so they looked all sharp and pointed.

'Don't you know who I am?'

I had hardly ever attempted an angrez accent. Mine sounded rather affected. The doorman blinked at me, baffled.

'Um . . . no?'

'Well, I,' I shrieked, my voice growing shriller with every syllable, 'am Mr Bhukhari's niece. And I say, it is rather unpleasant to be given this kind of a welcome home after three years of study in London.'

His flabby chin was shaking slightly as he attempted to form a coherent sentence.

'I didn't . . . he never . . . what niece?'

I rolled my eyes and put my hands squarely on my hips.

'Does he have some other thousand nieces for you to confuse me with?'

'No . . . I mean . . . not that I know of . . .'

'Look here, my plane just came in and I'm *exhausted*. So while I go inside to meet my uncle, *you* may kindly make me a cup of tea. English breakfast, please. Not kehva.'

With his mouth hanging open, he then gathered himself up enough to manage a, 'I . . . yes . . . of course, right away . . . please go right in . . .'

He shuffled around to the back of the building to get some tea ready, looking like he'd just survived a bomb blast. I nearly felt sorry for him.

Once his hulking frame had disappeared round the corner, I stepped inside the building. It was a maze of narrow passageways and low ceilings. For all its show, it was really quite small.

Chapter Eight

The door handle jerked and creaked as I turned it, so that I had to push hard. I entered the main office. It seemed frigid, though not in terms of temperature. Every surface was stiff and terrified, as though the slightest movement would give them away. Although indeed, I found myself shivering slightly; none of the gleaming heaters, stuffed unceremoniously into the walls at corners of the room, were on. The only source of natural light, of *any* light really, was a small window peering inquisitively at me from the upper-left corner of the room. It was as though the window had somehow needed to be fitted in despite no one really wanting it, so it had been crammed into where it would be least noticed.

I stared about in astonishment. A large, ornate desk was rooted in the centre of the room. I walked over to it. A few perfectly ruffled papers sat weary amidst glossy new pens, pencils, a bowl of vapid flowers and a table lamp. I touched the flowers with a tentativeness I've come to associate with testing the bathwater, expecting them to be made of plastic. But they felt real enough, if slightly dry and brittle. The surface of the desk was smooth to touch yet troubled beneath.

Acting on pure impulse, I put my ear to the surface and heard what sounded like miners thundering away at the inside of the table, surrounded by heat and noise and flame.

I pulled away, shifting one of the shiny grey pens slightly, and turned my glazed gaze to the bookshelves. Every book was black, perfectly bound and sealed shut, as though none had ever been opened. In seamless gold lettering they proclaimed the year they'd recorded, all arranged in chronological order.

As I moved closer to read what it was they documented, my eyes caught a sudden glint towards the back of the office. It was gone almost as quickly as it had come; I moved closer, my curiosity piqued, yet on guard.

A globe, seemingly attempting to be as large as what it represented, came slowly into view. It lay in the shrunken ray of light emerging from the dilapidated window. Splotches of a deep forest green displayed land, and shifting waves of clear turquoise, speckled with the occasional shipwreck or sea serpent, the oceans. The dust coating its dented surface could not yet hide its lost splendour; beneath the grime, it had once gleamed. Black, lacy letters sprawled across the map proclaimed the names of various countries. My eye caught on to a small copper latch in the Central Pacific. It must've been this that had shimmered through the bookshelves and demanded my attention. I traced the sunken grooves within it, and all at once, the globe popped open like a bottle cork, displacing the layers of filth upon it.

Holding its top half above me, I looked inside. Its interior was pearly white, like a chicken's egg, and completely hollow. Wondering whether I might find a hidden passage to an alternate universe in which my house was mine, my life was simple and the quill could sustain a normal conversation for more than a second or two, I leaned further in.

The handle of the door shuddered loudly. The door swung widely, forcefully open.

Startled by the sudden noise, I threw myself inside the globe. It nearly closed above me; I had prised my fingers into the gap just in time, and they smarted terribly as the top half of the globe closed on and collided with them. I squeezed my eyes shut in pain and annoyance. Why had I done that? All I had needed was to meet Mr Bhukhari, and there he was! But now I'd spoilt my chances by being stupidly impulsive! I was sure he hadn't seen me, and I couldn't just come leaping out from inside his globe demanding an audience; he'd probably have me thrown out! And then that poor doorman wouldn't get his pay.

I stayed where I was, grumbling inwardly and staring out through the gaps between my fingers. He marched in with the air of an army general surveying his troops, and I raised my eyebrows at his loud footsteps and marching gait. How self-important could one man get? Just then, my nostrils contracted at a potently repulsive smell, emanating from Mr Bhukhari. It was as though a decaying corpse had slipped its way inside of him and left its lingering stench upon his body. Disgusted, I grimaced at the odour, holding my free hand above my mouth to keep myself from coughing, wondering where on earth it could be coming from. He wore a box-shaped black cap, which seemed to me to be welded from the darkest metal, for it never once changed its sturdy shape. It matched the colour of his beady eyes perfectly. They shot back and forth, as though ensuring that no speck of dust had been swept away in his absence. He then placed his hat on his impeccable desk, revealing his sudden shock of white hair. I shook my head. It couldn't be natural; it didn't look anything like Tathi's hair. But why anyone would colour their hair to make themselves look *older* was a mystery to me. His pale translucent skin was blackened at the edges, beneath his nails and flesh, as though he was rotting from the inside out.

    He strode over to the door and it slipped meekly shut. I caught a quick glimpse of his face, and was surprised to find it a storm of emotions. Everything about him seemed tense and jittery. When he locked it, I began to feel uneasy. I didn't want to be encroaching upon something private; perhaps he was going to sit and cry about something. That's what I did whenever I felt like throwing a tantrum. I'd bawl in my room for a few minutes, during which Ma would be sensible enough to leave me well alone. After that I'd be quite all right again. Anyway, it's highly embarrassing to watch any stranger cry. What would a politician cry about, I wondered. An election lost? A policy not pushed through? A big loss in funds, or something of the sort?

    I allowed it to puzzle me for a moment. Then I realized he was not crying. On the contrary, he had seated himself at his desk in a most businesslike fashion, as though waiting for someone. He tapped his fingers together, straightened a pen that had been out of place, put on the table lamp, squinted, put it off again, started, and then stared down at the pen he'd put back in place. I forgot about keeping my nose pinched shut against the smell. My heart drummed like a tribal beat and I twisted my fingers sharply together while muttering furiously, 'Please . . . please don't notice . . . uh-oh . . . don't notice . . .'

My foot skidded against the curved surface of the sphere, and it swivelled slightly in its golden holder.

He looked around. His eyes fixed on the globe. He made to rise—

And there came a voice, a terrible, rusting voice, a voice that sounded like claws against cracking glass, the scream of a helpless mother as her child succumbed to the fever, the scrape of a blade against metal, the strangled cry of a fallen soldier, abandoned in the blood-soaked, dark, muddy battlefield.

I am ready.

Mr Bhukhari stumbled back into his chair, his lips pressed together, as though uttering a silent prayer. He sat so still that I wondered if he had been paralysed as I was. My head whipped around, searching for demons concealed in the wood, lungs yanking in great gulps of air, so frightened that I did not care if he heard me. A sudden, raw impulse begged me to call out to him to run, before sprinting out of the door myself. But I was behind that massive desk, with half the earth on top of me, and there was no way to leave fast enough to escape.

He tilted his head very slightly to the left, and it was then that I noticed a scramble of black veins, like worms, underneath his skin. They writhed and hissed, threatening to break through his pale, thin flesh. His breathing was coming in deep, loud bursts, his neck lolling uselessly—as though it had broken—his eyes fighting to stay open. Watching him, I almost closed my own. What was wrong with him? Why didn't he run?

I felt a sharp, nauseating pull in my abdomen and tried to look away. But I was frozen, unable to even blink as something sickeningly, horrifically lifeless, rotting and foul began to seep out of his ear and trickle on to the floor. The fetor of decay became thick and stale in the air . . . the lingering stench of an abandoned graveyard. It moved like a slug, sticking and sliming against all that touched it, sliding down the side of his lavish chair. All at once, the hot, stuffy air of the room became unbearable.

My heavily beating heart nearly tore itself out of my chest, then stopped entirely with a sudden jerk as the creature—no, the monstrosity . . . no, the devil itself—began to speak again, in a sinister, steady voice that seemed to come from nowhere in particular and yet everywhere at once. The gush of thick, black sludge slunk about the desk.

I have . . . begun to strengthen. You have done well.

Mr Bhukhari let out a ragged breath, and when he spoke, it seemed to cost him great effort. 'I have done . . . exactly as you asked. But I . . . I have requests too. And I want to make sure that you will see to it that . . . that they are fulfilled.'

Have I not completed these petty conditions of yours? You wanted power. You wanted influence. I have given you both already.

'No!' gasped Mr Bhukhari. Something in his pitiless black eyes hardened and blocked out any light. Was it determination? I shuddered. 'You haven't! You promised me that you would make me something akin to a god! That I would be the one to give my home what it has always deserved!'

His eyes shone with the heat of sickness.

'Its independence.'

His breaths came in gasps and gulps; the idea alone had left him breathless.

'You said everyone across India would know my name, that army troops would follow my every move! You vowed to change my irrelevance, the irrelevance of this land I'm forced to bind myself to, to break us off from that parasitic country we are forced to call home, to stop our degradation. You said my military would—'

Be quiet. Do you think I have forgotten? Enough.

Mr Bhukhari cringed as though he'd been slapped; yet the creature hadn't even raised its voice.

'I . . . I'm not your slave . . . I can speak . . .' He trailed off. The silence hung heavy in the air, pressing down upon me, crushing any hint of noise.

Yes.

It sounded amused.

I will explain once again. In choosing your body to inhabit, in binding myself to your pathetic mortal form, in using you as a concentration of myself, I've given you a greater power than you, a human, could ever hope to have.

My power.

'You haven't as much power as you say you have!' Mr Bhukhari lashed out. 'If you did, you'd never have needed to ask for my help in the first place, would you?'

A hiss, terrible, loathsome, sending petrifying fear across the room like a gas, pierced the walls before dripping slowly to the floor.

I bit my cheek so hard I tasted blood.

You dare ... hmm ... as it is I have felt you fight my control. No more. If I ask you to take action, you will trust that I have reason. My intelligence and prowess are far greater than yours, that you need not doubt, and I will not have you interfering.

And when it spoke again, I could sense a hint of carefully controlled anger in its repulsive voice.

You will bring me what I asked for, human. Or you will face the consequences. I take it we are not far from acquiring it?

'N-no,' he squeaked, frightened at last. 'I've ... the deal has been signed ...'

And I will give you what you ask for in return. My rise will be great and terrible. You need have no doubts about that.

'Doubts about what?' asked the politician quietly.

If grief is capable of joy, if death is capable of life, if sin is capable of repentance, then I suppose what I heard next could be called laughter.

So already you grow tired of our game? Only at our second meeting? Despite the fact that you have even denied me access to your mind?

'I'm not growing tired of anything. I just want my fair share.'

The sinewy shape at Mr Bhukhari's feet rose then, and like a thousand rotting fingers, it twisted upwards, wrapping the wood, pulling against the flowers. It engulfed them with the quiet hiss of smoke. Almost liquid, it sank to the floor like oil. As it came away from the flowers, it turned a shade darker with a sudden ripple, a snakeskin discarded and remade. And the flowers were then black, putrid and utterly dead. I finally found the impulse to squeeze my eyes shut. Still I could hear the dull crack of fallen petals. Still I could smell the repulsive scent of decay lingering upon my sweaty skin.

You see?

The voice was sickeningly triumphant. Mr Bhukhari said nothing.

Not yet, but soon . . . very soon . . . I will be powerful enough . . . my reign has not ended . . . it never had. Already with the help of your body I have grown. Already I've been chipping away into the heart of this merry, magical place . . .

It spat the last few words, so that its voice became a snarl.

I can almost . . . almost sense it in here . . . beneath this vile building's thick soapy scent . . .

Mr Bhukhari cleared his throat. I wondered how he dared to breathe.

See it as an act of kindness, will you not? Helping a poor, forgotten creature, a revenant, become a ruler once again. Is it not so very generous of you to aid in my rebirth?

'I don't want to be kind to you!' Mr Bhukhari burst out. He spoke the next words roughly, as though they had been forcibly wrenched through the walls of his heart, yet he spoke so quietly that I dared to hope the creature hadn't heard him. 'Kind people die alone.'

It gave a raspy cackle of appreciation.

That is why I chose you, of course. I see . . . how to put it . . . potential in you.

The sharp, clipped ring of the telephone shattered the stunned spell. My eyes were wrenched open painfully.

Mr Bhukhari snatched at it wildly, so that for a moment I was almost sure he was going to knock it off the table.

The shape rose then, a blackness so complete and endless that the dingy window found itself extinguished, eclipsed. Without a hint of warning, it slammed sideways into Mr Bhukhari's fragile skull, through his rotting ear.

Mr Bhukhari's bellow masked my sharp cry as the darkness, an insidious poison, entered him once again. He just sat at his desk, his teeth gritted and his fists clenched as his veins seemed to twist and wriggle beneath his skin. His hair flashed a brighter, more artificial shock of white. I fought the gasp threatening to escape from deep within my lungs and felt my skin grow colder at the creature's disappearance.

Then, shaking, he raised the telephone to his ear.

'Hello? Yes. Well. No. Yes. Fine. Now. Got it.'

He slammed the phone down, as though he could not have endured another syllable.

I watched him helplessly, feeling the most savage of sharp tears sting my eyes. It was just as the armchair had said . . . bitterness and blanketing rage . . . fuelled by humiliation and death. And yet his wish was the wish of many; often it was my own. I wanted so much to pat him heartily on the back, open all the doors and windows, and promise him that there was light at the end of this tunnel, that it hadn't caved in.

But I couldn't.

Twitching, grim, his feet planted firmly on the ground, he rose, moving slowly and cautiously towards the door.

The moment it shut behind him, I threw back the lid of the globe and took in a great, shuddering gulp of abruptly cool air. My chest stung sharply, and I swallowed, wincing. I counted thrice to twenty, listening hard, before deeming it safe to move. As soon as I gave myself permission to rise, my muscles erupted in a fury, launching me out of the hollow sphere towards the doorway like tightly coiled springs bursting free at last.

Mr Bhukhari was blinking rapidly in the glazed sunshine. I wished he would hurry up and leave. I was getting very cramped behind the front door, watching him from above one of the squeaky hinges. A new doorman, one I hadn't seen before, was helping him on to the tonga. The horse, a brilliant brown specimen with a thick, black mane, was whinnying nervously and stamping its hooves on the rocky ground. Its rider didn't really seem to care; he was far more occupied with keeping his squinted eyes on the leather pouch hooked to the politician's belt.

'But I tell you,' Mr Bhukhari was saying, 'I don't have a niece.'

From somewhere to my right, though I couldn't see him at all, I heard the doorman I'd spoken to respond.

'Arre, sahib! She was just here! I spoke to her! You . . . you must have some sort of relative like that, sahib.' Mr Bhukhari had finally succeeded in seating his large rear on the scratchy seat.

'I don't even have siblings. Where will a niece come from, you idiot?'

'But—'

The doorman who'd just finished helping Mr Bhukhari turned abruptly around and gave the poor fool the most dreadful evil eye I've ever seen.

'He said he didn't, now stop bothering sahib!'

There was silence from my right.

The horse was given a sharp smack. It neighed indignantly, hoping for acknowledgement, and when it got none, trotted off. The moment its relentless clattering faded out of earshot, the debate burst out again.

'Look here, my friend, I tell you I'm not mad.'

'You're entirely mad! Seeing girls where they don't exist! Irritating sahib like that! He very nearly forgot to give me a tip because of you!'

I tilted my head to see them both. He looked rather like a spoilt, chubby toddler sulking in the corner, but at least he didn't offer a rebuttal. He just sat down on a cluster of rocks, looking thoroughly bewildered by the day's events.

'Now,' continued his colleague in a calmer manner. 'There was no one here and we've settled that. But since you've made some tea, hand it over.'

The road had never felt this long. I turned around; gone were the spiny prickles of the bushes. And yet the hint of deep brown, of the sturdy, rough wood that had been shoved into place as a door, was nowhere to be seen. I suddenly wondered if this was endless; some sort of trap to keep me there till I grew old. It couldn't be, I reassured myself; all things have some kind of an end. This had a beginning. It will have an end.

Despite the reasoning suggested by my common sense, I tore down the path, lungs bursting. My heart pumped harder than ever in fear.

Finally I skidded to a halt. After dusting myself off a bit (Tathi can be a stickler about looking decent), I moved to open the door. And froze.

The handle was hanging off its hinge. The top window was completely cracked, hundreds of darkened splinters weaving through the glass, so that it looked ready to shatter with the first gust of wind.

Something small and hard hit my shoulder and I gasped involuntarily. I peered down at it, rubbing the place it had struck, expecting it to be a pebble. But it was a deep brown, with pointed edges. Brick? I looked up. The roof seemed to have altered into a jumbled maze of materials. Leaks that I'd never known to exist had been plugged up with broken bricks, a bucket, and a comb with three snapped-off teeth. The entire roof seemed to be tilting over on its side, about to flop down on the ground. Each tile was quivering with the tension of holding everything together.

I couldn't, for the life of me, remember the secret knock. I rammed all of my small body against the door. It didn't budge, staring coolly back at me. I began pounding away at the door with every limb I had.

'Tathi! Tathi! Open the door right away! I need help! We all need help! Hurry!'

The door was slowly pulled open, as though there was all the time in the world. Which really could not have been further from the truth.

There, in the doorway, was Tathi, looking older than all of her worries had ever made her. Her hair had thinned considerably, her eyes and cheeks had hollowed, and she rested heavily on her walking stick, weight still pressing down on her bad knee. Her stubby fingers seemed red and sore and her bones screeched when she moved.

Worst of all, she wasn't smiling. That's how you know when someone's joy has been frayed by life's grinding rituals. Their smile gets smaller and smaller until it becomes a sad, droopy little thing, only used at family gatherings and seldom even then.

'Tathi?' I began, unsure how to proceed.

She stared at me for a long while. When she spoke, I could barely understand her.

'Come in, Zoons. There's something I must tell you. Something that perhaps you've already sensed, and is more a part of you than you could have ever known,' she rasped huskily.

The beanbag seemed more uncomfortable than usual. I leaned down to check for rips at the sides. 'Zoon,' came Tathi's voice, and I looked up sharply. 'What I'm about to tell you is not at all to be shared with your mother. Understand? That woman has seen enough suffering as it is.'

I nodded vehemently.

'I'm sure you've realized by now that there is something unusual about our house.'

I nodded again, and for a little too long; it seemed to call for a more forceful response, but I didn't know what to say.

'There is magic within it, because long ago it was made magic by our oldest and wisest ancestor. It was made for a specific purpose. To battle something called . . .'

I tuned out as she continued. People do have a tendency to rant when speaking of something they're passionate about; it's most irritating. In that moment, however, it was quite welcome. My eyes darted about, surveying all the damage. It was as though wild animals had attacked every square inch they could get at. All the cabinets were hanging crooked, most suspended by a single hinge. The whistling of the winter wind came clearly through the kitchen; one or two of the windows had surely been smashed through already. The stuffing was hanging out of the side of Tathi's armchair. My foot crunched down on splintered glass, and I wondered where it had come from. One or two of the pieces were tinged with red; that explained Tathi's fingers.

Just when I thought she had finished, she began again.

'And now, I'm sure you'd like to understand what happened to your father.'

I opened my mouth to say no, that there was no need, I'd been told already. Then I saw that her eyes were glistening, threatening to spill salty rivers of grief. My heart gave a guilty twinge. There she was, pouring out the darkest parts of her damaged soul to me, and I wasn't even paying attention.

'Your great-grandfather was terminally ill. He was Guardian for twenty-six miserable years. The Guardian protects the heart of Kashmir; as he falls, so falls everything that a heart contains: love, unity, our culture, our hopes, our blessings . . . No one was safe. People tried to flee the riots and the chorus of showering bombs. But even when the dust settled, when Kashmir was ripped apart, when our people had been murdered and thrown out to the vultures, those that remained left to desolation and disease, no one could forget what had happened. It was in their eyes.'

I had started when she began to speak, so suddenly was this information thrown upon my unsuspecting mind. 'And is this . . .' I began, hesitant to interrupt yet curious. 'Is this your father's fault?'

She gave a tight smile. 'If you were younger, I would have said yes. But you are old enough to know by now that it is never that simple.'

I fell silent. Yes, I did know. There was always one fault that led to another, always one blame to be fitted into another, so much so that all the mistakes I'd ever made could somehow be traced back to the greed of the demon king.

It seemed that Tathi could not continue. Her worn face was buried in her hands, and the rest of her was not very far from being buried either. She fought, as she always has, to go on.

'And then . . . once he passed away . . . your father stepped up . . . and said that he'd be a much stronger . . . better Guardian . . . determined to be what his grandfather hadn't been . . . and that very thought consumed . . . him . . .'

I couldn't bear to hear her tell the story any more. Even if I hadn't known all the rest already, I could see it gave her too much grief for me to remain silent.

'Tathi, please. You don't have to continue. I know this part of the story already.'

She looked up, startled.

'How? Surely your mother doesn't know? If she does, I must speak to her at once. All these years, she never—'

'No, no. She doesn't. It was the armchair. He told me.'

Her body, if such a sack of skin and bone could truly be called that any more, visibly relaxed. She twisted her fingers around her wrist, as though wondering about a missing bangle.

'But,' she whispered huskily, 'he does not know all of it either.'

I leaned forward, though I could hear her just fine. Grasping her calloused hands, I nodded at her gently to continue.

'No one knows all of it,' she went on, 'except for me. And now you.'

She took a shaky breath, and it sounded as though it had been fighting to pass through a sliver of a windpipe.

'The house believes that his arrogance was his downfall. But Kruhen Chay did not just kill your father. I only wish it had been that peaceful. Zoon, Kruhen Chay does a great deal more than physical harm. He infests minds and hearts with grief, ensnares people's thoughts and dreams until he drives them insane. And only then, once they have been torn apart from the inside out, does he murder them. In your father, Kruhen Chay sensed a bit of himself. He realized that this was a Guardian whom he could use rather than fight. And he wormed his way into your father's mind, feasting on his belief that he could completely control the house's power. Which I had warned him he could not.'

Tathi began to deteriorate once more. It was like watching a music box spinning round and round and round, believing itself meaningful, beautiful, yet always ending up where it started again and never knowing what happened in between.

'Did I not tell him enough? Did I not beg my son to stay away, just stay away, it was all too much for him to take . . . not so young . . .'

She looked up at me, her eyes tinged a harsh, scraped red, with no tears to cool their grief. I nodded slowly.

'You told him. You told him everything. You were not, and have never been, inadequate. Tathi, you must stop blaming yourself for his death.'

'But I cannot find peace—all of these years, gone in second-guessing myself. I have prayed, I have hoped, I have laboured, and for what?'

'Peace,' I replied, 'is not found. It is recognized.'

She fell silent, slowly leaning back in her rickety chair.

I badly wanted her to tell me more, yet I pressed myself to stay silent, to wait till she seemed ready.

When she spoke again, her voice was steadier, and her rasp seemed to have worn away.

'And so it went. Kruhen Chay infiltrated your father's mind. And as Kruhen Chay gained in strength, your father became no longer an obstacle, but a doorway. And when he was murdered, their Guardian crushed, the house feared that their enemy had finally won.'

'They believe it was a miracle that saved them, a burst of magic from the Guardian's utter defeat,' I put in, eager to show her that I understood, I knew, I was with her. 'They say they've not had a Guardian since.'

She smiled then, for the first time since I had seen her today. 'It was no miracle. I suppose the armchair told you this; he tends to overdramatize things. No, it was me.'

'You?' I gasped. 'What do you have to do with it?' A laugh, a real laugh, came spiralling from her throat.

'My dear Zuzu, have you forgotten that I too am from the Razdan bloodline? I was the one who was meant to take over after my father when he passed. But my son rose too soon, before me. And he barely lasted ten years . . . after which I, of course, took the reins.'

I was trying to drink it all in. It seemed like a bitter medicine I had to swallow, but every time I tried I would retch.

'So . . .' I began, trying to untangle her words as they mashed themselves over each other in my brain, screaming and getting into fist fights.

'You've been the Guardian ever since my dad passed. You're the one who . . . kept all the bad stuff out . . . right?'

She took her glasses off and cleaned them slowly and deliberately with the edge of her dupatta. It was the first time I'd ever seen her clean them. I watched her as she brushed away the layers of filth that had gathered over the years, until all that remained was a sturdy sheet of glass. She made sure that they had gripped firmly behind her ears before speaking again.

'I couldn't bear to live in the house any more. So I moved here. It is close, but far enough away that the ghosts can't reach me. Or so I thought.'

Two thoughts catapulting over each other in my brain collided and merged.

'So that's why you never come over!' I whispered furiously. She gave me the tiniest of nods. Whom were we hiding this from, I wondered. The neighbours? The quiet evening? Ourselves?

'I pushed myself, because I wanted to do whatever I could to help my son in death.' Her voice grew louder. 'Protect his family. And I tried, Zoon. I wanted to keep you both safe and happy and blessedly ignorant. I have not spoken with the house in years, but from what you have told me, I believe we both had the same goal. We never wanted to see you crumple beneath the burden we have all faced before you. We never wanted you to be forced to become our Guardian.'

Finally, a hidden teardrop slid down her withered cheeks. Perhaps it was her last. The culmination of fifteen years of grief: a single tear.

'But now,' she went on as her voice threatened to crack under the strain, 'now I fear I can stop it no longer.'

My stomach plunged to the ground, and I felt hollow and nauseated all at once. At that moment, it seemed that my appetite would never return.

'Why not?'

'Because you'll be fifteen tomorrow, Zoon. And fifteen is the coming-of-age for any Guardian. I can't hold on to the power any more. The magic is flowing to you, despite my best efforts. I have felt myself grow weaker; I dreaded what it meant.'

'And Kruhen Chay has grown stronger.' My tongue twisted around itself in fright at the name, so that I fought to continue speaking. 'I know. I've felt it.'

Tathi nodded sagely. 'Of course you have. As have I. The weaker the Guardian, the stronger the enemy. And I'm afraid I haven't been up to scratch lately, Zuzu.'

'No, but there's another reas—' I cut off abruptly, my train of thought having been stopped in its tracks by reason.

I had gone there to tell Tathi what I had seen. I had gone there to shift some of my burden on to her. Indeed, all I ever did when presented with a burden was find someone to pass it on to. The armchair, the fireplace, my mother . . . but then, Tathi had ended up relieving her burden on me. I saw how much she had needed that. I was not going to be the one to burden her again. I would not be able to live with myself if I did. I took a deep, calming breath. It did little to calm me.

'So I have to stop Kruhen Chay by becoming the Guardian?' She nodded, eyes wide and glazed over, hands contorted in her lap.

'On your fifteenth birthday, the energy must flow to you. Or the house will indeed be destroyed, Zoon, and the magic of Kashmir—or whatever is left—will be snuffed out forever.'

'We can't let that happen,' I replied. 'We can't let the darkness win.'

I found a very interesting pebble in the dirt on the way home. It was slim and slender, shaped so smoothly that I marvelled at nature's craft. It gleamed black from amongst the others, unafraid to jut out or be stepped upon, bold and velvet, like the night. Indeed, I had been on the verge of picking it up. But it was only when I knelt closer to it that I realized it was far too metallic to be a pebble. And it was only when I scooped it up, turning it over in my filthy fingers, that I realized it had never been a pebble at all, but a bullet shell.

A vicious fury seethed inside my stomach and, suddenly, I despised everything about that little object in my palm. I could never have said why this frustration hit me so profoundly at that precise second. I pulled my arm so far back that I felt my muscles tremble with the strain, and launched that silly black blob of rusting copper into the air. It had barely left the caress of my fingertips when I was blasted into the air just behind it.

I hit the ground with a sudden jolt of pain, which then dulled, spread out and sank deep into my aching limbs. I felt the bullet press into my cheek, cool and merciless. Along my spine, I felt the light touch of burning hail. I looked over my shoulder and saw flames, like a distant sun, searing against my home. Amidst the roars, the bangs, the crackling of feet against the road, I strained to hear the beating of my own heart.

Mothers fled, knowing full well that there was nowhere to go, their children sobbing about lost siblings and oozing red wounds and dinner.

Men cried words of warning, of help, of chaos, of anger. A thick black demon was unfurling itself against the melting carmine sky, flame pouring from its gaping maw. The onlookers made to drag their families from the blaze. Their yells echoed against brick so that the cries of the dying mingled in the air with the cries of the living, till neither was even vaguely different any more. Chunks of gravel and metal the size of my palm were smouldering down from the skies. Blackness began to drift lazily across the land and people choked, vomiting from the thick, dark gas. My eyes darted spastically, fighting to find a familiar face, a boy's rumpled deep brown hair and a thin, bone white cap.

Across the street from me, the tongewala had deposited a small bent figure with shrunken, useless limbs. His body had turned a sunken, hollow black, shredded at the edges. His face, I assumed, was turned away from me. I couldn't really tell, for his head was a raw, mangled mass of blood-soaked flesh and bone. It clashed horribly with the dirt-filled brown of the road. Vaguely, my mind questioned whether his left leg had always been missing.

Every part of me throbbed as though swollen already, ready to burst crimson at the slightest provocation. Yet I dared to imagine that I was mostly unhurt. For it was only when oxygen returned in great gulps that the burning under my right eye began to sink in. And it was only when I looked straight down at the sea of rock again and realized it was tinted a sick, bright red, clustered around the dense, unmoving bullet, that I lifted my hand to register the gash on my muddy cheek, my blood finally becoming one of the puddles I'd so tried to avoid.

Chapter Nine

People tell me that you never need to worry about being able to find your way home. I couldn't understand them in the least; did they mean I'd never get lost? Did they mean those I could love and trust would always surround me? Or did they mean that my heart would always eventually guide me to happiness? Or perhaps they meant all of those things at once?

Right then, it was swirling about in my mind, over and over, like the clanging of pots and pans in a soapy sink when my mother does the dishes.

I was walking, just walking, pushing through the smoke and fog, forcing myself not to panic by focusing on the irrelevant. Around me, there were calls for help, for warning, for God. I had fled from where the men with guns began to pour in from brash, hulking brown jeeps. Fleetingly, I had longed to question whose side they were on. Then I realized it did not matter. They were holding guns. Something animalistic inside me had risen to the surface and propelled me through the smallest of hidden cracks and keyholes to set me on the track home. Or what I believed was the track home. I did not know.

People rushed away from the site of the blast as I had, hoping for nothing more than preserving a fraction of what had been their life. A wooden sign, shattered and splintering, crunched beneath my shaking feet, bearing a discoloured C. Chana.

Only the old men seemed unchanged. They watched as the road and the air grew red, as the wounded were brought away and uselessly bandaged, as chaotic gunshots calling for order echoed in the evening, and they sat and read their newspapers on the front porch with the same indifferent look in their eyes.

Such was the flow of familiar unfamiliarity that I did not even notice when I reached my road. Men and women swarmed around me, some going one way, some the other, some not moving at all. Then I felt a firm hand grip my arm, and I was yanked up and out of it all.

'Thank all the gods you're okay!' Ma panted as she held me against her on the front steps. 'Oh, no!' she murmured when she saw my face, worry and care misting around her. She tilted my chin this way and that, trying to quickly ascertain the damage.

'Is everyone else . . .?' I whispered, thinking of the houses I had passed, and which of them Rani Auntie might have been in, or worse, the Alis, so hoarse that I went unheard.

Past her arm, something black and deformed was lingering like a disease in the pores of the soil. Ancient cracks splintered through maggot-infested wood; bare, dead branches, contorted like amputated limbs, hung limply in the chilly air; a small, parasitic flame loitered wickedly within the crevices of decay. And my stomach contracted, filling my thin, white-veined lungs with nausea at the thought of how much of the tree was yet living.

'Ma,' I croaked, 'our chinar.'

She clicked her tongue impatiently as she caught me by the elbow and spun me around to face the door, muttering something about priorities.

Mr Qureshi was seated in the living room, looking as though the bomb had just exploded two inches from his enormous nose. His eyes were wide and he was clutching his briefcase with the air of a drowning man gripping a torn lifebelt. On the desk beside him, a crackly old radio that I'd never seen before was belching out a long blurred sentence.

Ma marched me upstairs immediately and began to wash my face with a wet cloth. Once all the blood had been wiped away, she sighed.

'There. It's not so bad, is it? It isn't a deep wound at least.'

Right, Ma. Sure it isn't.

'Listen to me,' she barked, suddenly anxious. 'Don't you see now, Zoon? Don't you understand why we can't live here any more? The armies are fighting at the border, in the *city*, as we speak! That bomb in Nowhatta will be the first of many more now. Much worse could have happened to you. I don't know what your poor Tathi would have done if—'

She stopped and stared at a moth on the mirror.

'Your poor Tathi!' she cried suddenly, shoving me aside.

Halfway to the door, she paused and turned.

'I'm going to get Tathi. Don't touch your cut. Don't go downstairs. Stay in your room, lock the door, don't be too loud, and don't answer to anyone unless you hear me come in. Mr Bhukhari is waiting in the living room to sign the papers and I am dealing with far too much right now to have to endure any nonsense from you as well. Got it?'

My head seemed to nod of its own accord.

As she stumbled down the stairs, I heard Mr Qureishi give a frightened yelp.

'Those men are getting closer! Look, they're halfway here already! You know, I . . . I really think I ought to leave! Listen, Mrs Razdan, it isn't that I don't want to help with the sale. I do. But I'm afraid to say that I've decided to place higher value on my life as of now than on my business. It may sound ridiculous, but there it is. I hope you don't mind?'

'Of course not!' Ma replied, trying her hardest to pay attention while, by the sound of it, searching for her second shoe. 'You have somewhere to go, I suppose?'

'Yes, I'm headed to my aunt's. She lives a couple of minutes from here, over on Boulevard Road. She probably hasn't even realized what's going on, poor thing. Perhaps I can grab her and make a dash for it.'

The front door was thrown open dramatically, letting in small wisps of mist, and a clatter of footsteps preceded an eerie silence.

It was broken by the voices of the portraits erupting in hurried mutters. Even the emperor had lost his jovial grin in the wake of the imminent—I shuddered—battle. I felt as though I had missed a step going down the stairs, and my stomach had lodged uncomfortably in between my rapidly constricting ribcage.

'Dear,' came the voice of the empress. 'I think now is the time for me to recite this piece I've been—'

'Not now, lamb!' whispered the emperor, mortified. 'She wants you all to know,' he continued, louder, 'that she has lived here for over 200 years, and that in all her time she has never, and hence will never, see her home succumb to evil.'

This summary seemed, rather than saving time, to have led to an increase in the muttering. 'Very true, very true,' murmured the kisan, his eyes hooded and his head lolling on his shoulder. I doubted he had any idea what we were talking about.

'Listen, we're all with you!' called the Mughal warrior, pulling out his elegant blade, then staring about importantly, as though challenging someone to declare any form of cowardice.

'We . . . we are,' said the scribe, his eyes having dulled in their usual soothing glow. 'Fear can be a powerful manipulator. But you mustn't let it change the way you view yourself.'

He had lifted himself off his pile of dusty pillows and seemed to want to elaborate on this, but at that moment, one of the Pandits coughed pointedly. They all fell silent, staring at the back wall, some looking astonished, others eager and excited at this event; the Pandits had had rare cause to speak in the past.

'Zoon,' began the Pandit furthest to the left, my great-great-great-(I didn't even know how many greats)-grandfather. 'You know what's waiting down there. You know what you must do. You must do what I had done, so many, many years ago, and was foolish enough to believe no one would have to do again.'

'There will always be a sign,' croaked a Pandit towards the right, whose image was a faded black-and-white photograph. 'You will know when the time comes, and when it does, you mustn't hesitate.'

A flash of recognition stirred in my mind: Rahul Razdan, the first Guardian.

I didn't move from my spot on the bed. It seemed my bones were sinking into the mattress like it was quicksand.

'Listen,' cut in the only portrait printed in colour, speaking briskly and importantly, 'you're really all we have left at this point.'

I blinked at him, thrown by his matter-of-fact cynicism. It didn't do anything to calm my nerves, but before I could contemplate the matter thoroughly, voices had broken out again, some helpful, some chaotic, some frightening.

'But you must be careful!' came a voice from the middle of the wall. Soon I located the source: a sketch of an aged Pandit and his daughter. She had a rather wry look about her and did not move at all; it was almost as though she was part of the background. I wondered at how I had not noticed her before. My eyes shifted to the Pandit once again. His beard looked as though clumps had been torn out of it. His turban was unravelling at the end.

'I have seen what Kruhen Chay can do,' he continued. 'I have watched him lure an innocent British soldier into his clutches and murder him the moment he had fulfilled his purpose. I have watched him shatter every window of this house and set alight every pile of snow. He infects and inflames the homes of the valley; I know the devastation he can wreak on Kashmir, and with time there shall be nothing left for him to consume; you must be very careful.'

'You saw him murder someone?' I whispered, sickened. To hear of it was one thing, and that ghastly enough; to witness a man have the life ripped from his feeble, frozen fingers was another thing entirely.

The Pandit nodded grimly.

'And I was killed the very next day,' he muttered. 'Luckily I'd hidden my daughter in the broom cupboard . . . and taught her well enough to see that she kept him out . . . she took over . . . and she'd learnt well . . . perhaps I was too harsh on her then . . .'

'It doesn't matter how young you are,' regaled one of the watercolours, interrupting as always. His colours were deep and vibrant, his pheran a bright white amidst fluffy orange pillows. His beard had been painted a deep brown, unlike the others; I suspected that it was his youth that always compelled him to speak. 'What matters, in the end, is your strength of heart,' he finished masterfully, 'for it is that heart, and not your body, that is protecting us all.'

'So no pressure,' I muttered. 'Thanks.'

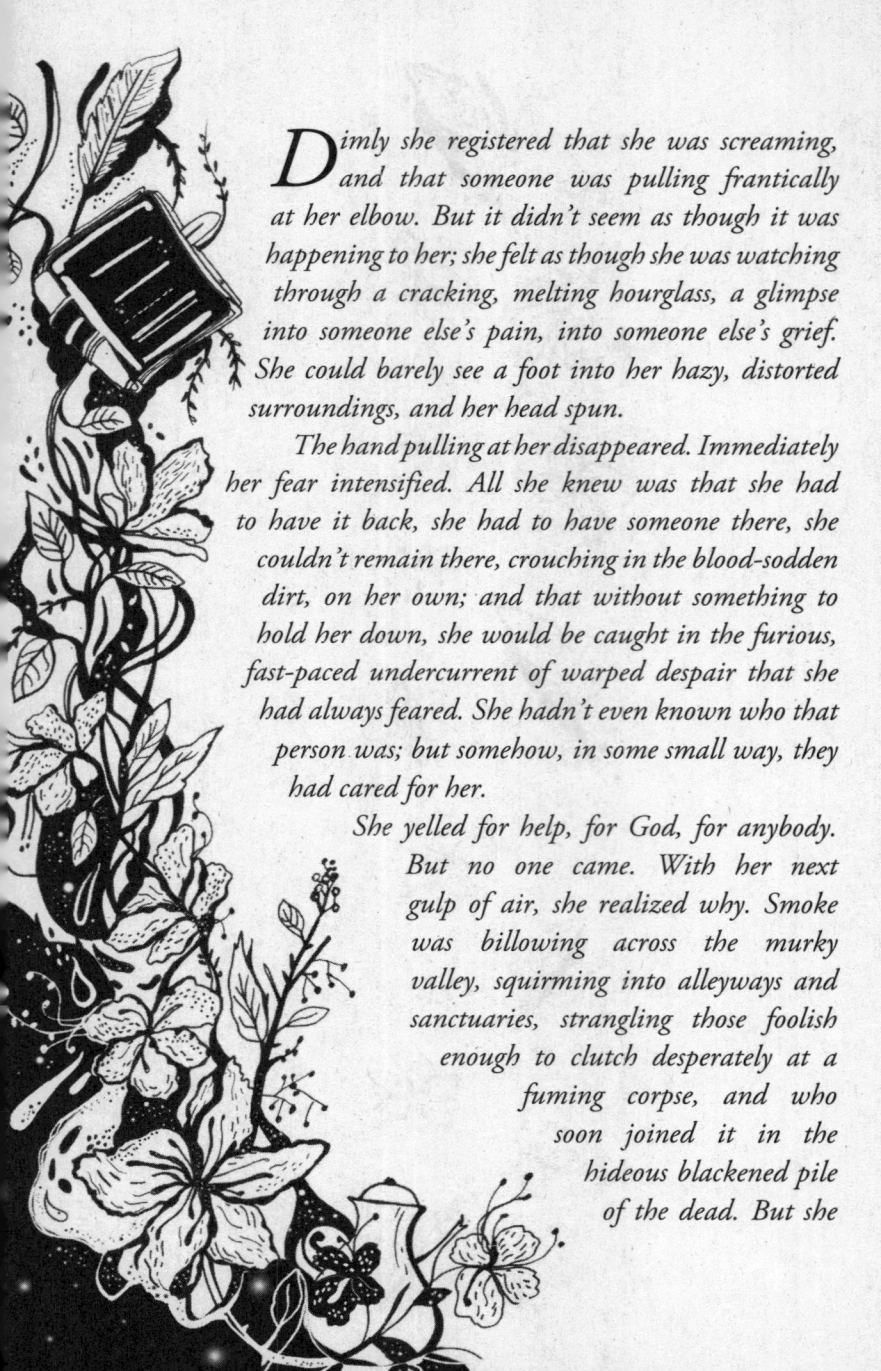

Dimly she registered that she was screaming, and that someone was pulling frantically at her elbow. But it didn't seem as though it was happening to her; she felt as though she was watching through a cracking, melting hourglass, a glimpse into someone else's pain, into someone else's grief. She could barely see a foot into her hazy, distorted surroundings, and her head spun.

The hand pulling at her disappeared. Immediately her fear intensified. All she knew was that she had to have it back, she had to have someone there, she couldn't remain there, crouching in the blood-sodden dirt, on her own; and that without something to hold her down, she would be caught in the furious, fast-paced undercurrent of warped despair that she had always feared. She hadn't even known who that person was; but somehow, in some small way, they had cared for her.

She yelled for help, for God, for anybody. But no one came. With her next gulp of air, she realized why. Smoke was billowing across the murky valley, squirming into alleyways and sanctuaries, strangling those foolish enough to clutch desperately at a fuming corpse, and who soon joined it in the hideous blackened pile of the dead. But she swore she would not be one of them. Not for herself, but for her daughter.

So Shanti planted a final kiss on the wrinkled forehead of her last loved elder, creating small rivulets of tears that ran down her still face, the only part of her saved from the charred rot caking her body. She lay unmoving, completely oblivious to this show of love. Her eyes were closed, but as though she had embraced death with open arms, as though she had known it was coming before it knew that itself. In a sudden gush of twisted desolation, Shanti almost laughed; she had died wearing her glasses. And after all these years, they had finally cracked.

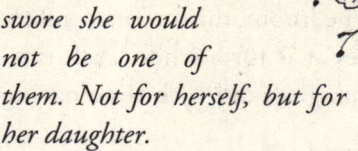

My eyes skittered up to the bedroom mirror once more. I'd been sneaking quick glances at it for a while, each time hoping to see something encouraging and each time having these hopes dashed.

My hair was a tangled mess. No one looking at me then would have been able to tell that I had a fringe. Bits of black were sticking out of my stumpy braid. The slash across my cheek looked as though it had been made with a chainsaw. I looked closer and noticed my shivering knees. I shut my eyes firmly, forcing out the grave overlapping mumbles of the portraits.

This isn't you.
But what if it is?
It isn't.
Says who?
Says me.
Who even *are* you?
. . . I'm you, but smarter.
That makes no sense. So I'm like a two-faced rakshasa or something?
I never said I had a face.
So you're an atma. I'm possessed. Perfect.
Zoon! Focus!
Sorry.

Tentatively, I let my eyelids slide open, petals on a blooming flower bud. The girl I saw in the mirror was tall and straight-backed. Her hair was thrown back over her shoulder in a jumble; people like her had no time for such things. She had the tiniest of scrapes across her cheek, no thinner than a mouse's whisker.

I put my hands on my hips.
So did she.
I took in a deep, long breath.
'Let's do this thing.'

The living room has never felt smaller than when I walked in to find Mr Bhukhari at its centre. The black in his eyes seemed to have swelled, so that he no longer resembled a human as much as a bloodsucking insect. With a twisted grin like that of a poorly made puppet, he leered at me, waving a smudged piece of crumpled paper in the air—the deeds to the house.

Just then, I heard a gentle dripping of thick, clear liquid against the front window. I turned to stare at it, all of me tensing, as though it might spontaneously combust.

I heard a gulp, and whipped around to see Mr Bhukhari staring rigidly at the bare ceiling pressing against the strain of the snow at its corners. He clutched his papers so tightly that I saw whatever blood he had left leave his skin; he dug his shoes into the carpet, as though afraid he would be blown away by the wind.

A gush of water brought us to our senses; outside, a waterfall was streaming down the window in thick sheets. Beyond it, the world was thick smog and jumbled shouts. I stared at it, transfixed, as the ridges and bumps in the window grew more pronounced beneath the crystal cascade, almost as though all the snow on the roof had melted in that sudden instant.

A sinister hissing erupted from the fireplace; I turned my head so fast I felt the muscles in my neck twinge with the pain.

Drops of water had splattered on to the embers in the grate, thick and round, leaping back at once in wisps of steam.

I made to push my hair out of my face, and my hand brushed against moist, clammy skin, slick with sweat. I let out a small, controlled pant, and sucked in a lungful of hot air.

And that's when I heard it—the gentle, elegant scrape of rusty claws against the inside of the chimney, accompanied by a foul smell that was growing dangerously familiar.

I leapt backwards as though I'd been burnt, my breathing becoming rapid and panicky, watching, listening as the sounds grew louder, punctuated by soft, dangerous hisses . . .

But nothing emerged.

And still nothing.

Mr Bhukhari let out a wild, fluctuating laugh, still smiling that horrible smile of his, with his mouth too full of teeth and his face a doughy mass of pale, lifeless flesh.

And then I felt an excruciating pain in my abdomen, so that I gasped and clutched at it, blind to everything else. My enemy's first strike. A harpoon had struck me straight through my stomach; I was the helpless, dying fish, flopping at the bottom of the boat.

'No!' roared a sharp, fiery cry.

And all at once, the fireplace burst into flame.

The pain in my stomach lessened slightly; I could think clearly again.

I'd never seen the fireplace come alight of his own accord before. I'd thought he couldn't manage it any more.

Somehow, his fire was brighter and greater than any we could ever have lit. Smoke began billowing steadily from the crackling logs, and yet not one wisp was allowed to squirm up into the chimney. The fireplace continued to dispense dollops of smoke, until it curved sinuously against the wood and moved to fill the living room. Inexplicably, despite the flames, the air had cooled slightly.

Gradually, like a buried fossil, a shape began to emerge before me, growing clearer every second. It was something akin to the silhouette of a man, but this monster was *nothing* like a man. He was large, so large that the splotch of misery meant to serve as his head was pushing up against the ceiling. Warped limbs and chunks of body parts emerged from every side of him, spasming and flailing as though they were still attached to their owners. Perhaps he had swallowed them whole . . . And one of them was my father's. I forced myself not to tremble.

All of him was a sickening, rotting black. But even in this black I could see the grotesque carvings of his past: a thousand decades, a thousand faces, a thousand screams. When he moved, the air around him rippled and distorted, so that it seemed like all the world was a crude, crumpled drawing, and he was a rip in the paper.

I should have destroyed that fireplace when I had the chance, he remarked coolly.

I flinched, but tried to alter it into a look of disgust. I couldn't let him see that his horrific, rasping voice, like the scrape of metal against rock, had nearly made my ears bleed.

All at once he winced terribly and let out something akin to a growl. Turning to the fireplace, I saw that melted snow was continuing to drip serenely from the chimney, and the rush of steam sizzling within the smoke had collided with his burnt surface.

I stared too long.

Without warning, he lunged.

Acting on pure instinct, I flung myself towards the wall, as though I were a corpse already, without any thought as to where or how I would land. Had it not been for the carpet, who rose up to catch me in the soft, interlaced weaves of her cloth, I would surely have cracked something against the floor.

The sudden ferocity of his attack alarmed me. Every nerve cell in my body was screaming instructions at my frozen brain.

When I turned to face him again, I found him leering at me from beside a smouldering crater he'd made in the wall. Again he struck, but I was ready and waiting, and I dodged him once more. A small flicker of triumph swept across my pumping heart, and it felt lighter than it had in a while. I was winning!

Then I heard him burst into a cackling roar of pleasure, and my heart sank immediately. Once more, I saw him push himself out of a crater he'd hewn from the wall. The wood had splintered horribly, and it began to go a darker brown than I'd ever seen it, a dying tree unable to reach the soil.

He was destroying the house.

My house.

And for every blow I dodged, it would suffer.

I did not move, yet he sensed that I had understood. A deep chasm carved into his face began to twist itself so that the ends curved upwards. He surveyed me as a cruel army general would survey his deadened enemy, weak and wounded before the might of his guns, waiting patiently to be blasted into nightmarish nothingness.

Out of nowhere, a spark of light catapulted towards Kruhen Chay like a firework. The log sizzled against the surface of his distorted form, and he let out a fierce cry that tore through the air like a million shards of broken glass, cutting through my skin. Slowly, his yells melted into a slippery hiss of anger.

But before either of us had time to fully recover, the fireplace launched another flaming log into the room. Kruhen Chay smacked it away from him, spitting furious insults, and it collided heavily with the fireplace's aged marble.

Rage curled his fingers into menacing claws. *You think your pathetic attempts will hinder me? I who have earned my power every step of the way!*

'What do you mean "earned your power"?' I replied bitterly. I felt my resolve beginning to grow again. 'You've brought nothing but misery to people, and I'm putting an end to it.'

With irritation, he turned a deeper black than ever, so that the only way I could keep track of him was by looking for that which I could not see.

Silly, impertinent girl. I have been here longer than your filthy race can fathom. I'll put an end to your chatter soon enough.

And he rose above the ground, readying himself for the attack.

I felt like a taut balloon, filled with too much air too quickly, on the verge of bursting from the pressure.

Just before I popped, my eyes latched desperately on to the twinkling glint of gold. My heart, pumping so adamantly and furiously a second before, seemed to have choked and stuttered to a stop. Because something was shimmering behind him, a myriad of delicate, glittering colours, precious uncut jewels glowing in the growing darkness. I couldn't look away. And, at that moment, I realized I had to reach them.

Without knowing what they meant, or what they were, or why they had appeared so suddenly in the dark, my mind trained on them, blocking out all else, and refused to relent to any reason.

I began, one thread of the carpet at a time, to move closer.

'So you weren't always this awe-inspiring?' I pressed, doing my best to distract him, stuttering from the effort to produce coherent speech. If I could just keep him talking . . .

Of course not. I was shadow.

'You were a shadow?'

Not a shadow, you fool. I was shadow. All shadows. And I despised it.

'Really? Why? That sounds like an interesting job!'

He seemed to swell with displeasure, his mouth twisted in seething anger.

It wasn't a job! It was punishment. I could not exist without another, without a living being. I was dependent on . . . light.

The darkness rippled, as though he had shuddered.

Getting nearer . . . but mustn't move too quickly . . . I was pressing forward, keeping my distance from master and servant alike . . .

But it mattered not, you see. Perhaps once, I needed light to exist. But now, I engulf this very light, I destroy it. You're just like the rest of your kind. So sure they were, when they brought in that flame, of their lovely bright future.

'Fire,' I whispered to myself. 'And that means you owed them, didn't it?'

He gave a feral snarl.

I went on, louder, 'For helping you to exist even at night? For letting you exist at all?'

I owe nothing!

The floor reverberated with the sudden force of his wrath, and I jerked back a step, feeling a sharp point like a shark's tooth under my bare feet. I looked down and saw small nails jutting out of each crevice in the wood. Parts of the floor had cracked and risen higher than the rest, the planks beneath me a suddenly stormy sea.

Without the blaze, I was nothing, and they controlled this . . . fire.

I was inching closer . . . but my frustration increased with every step; I needed him to move so that I could see past him . . .

His voice grew malicious and sinister, dangerously silky.

And yet, with the flames, they brought in a new realm of shadow, and I grew . . . I am a human's worst fear! I am built up of their misery and suffering, that which they will never overcome. I lord over them. I have taken everything from them as I will take now from you!

I saw it then. The split second in which he rose over me had been enough. I had seen it, and then I was sure. The crest was glowing. Mr Bhukhari, who was leaning heavily against the side of the fireplace, his eyes closed from the effort of staying alive himself, hadn't noticed anything.

And yet it was clear to me. The crest was made of precious stones that glittered and danced in the flame of the roaring fire. The swans were indeed a delicate pink, and spread their wings lovingly around the third, misty-grey swan against a royal purple. The light shimmered across them, and when it caught a particular tilt on the crest, I noticed that the three swans joined together in the shape of a palm.

I felt as though I, too, was glowing from the inside, as though a searing, red-hot iron had lit up the core of my soul. 'You won't!' I burst out at Kruhen Chay. 'You never have and never will be able to defeat those in whom our magic is strong!'

I thought fleetingly of Altaf, goofy, carefree and spontaneous. How foolish I'd thought him when we first met.

A malicious, warped, sickeningly mocking voice slid its coils around me and pulled me back to the present.

Like your father?

I opened my mouth to retaliate, but my brain was lagging behind, and I could think of nothing to say.

He was so strong he didn't even need to wait till he was of age, did he? Ah, it is always so simple. He thought he was destined to be a king, and let me lurk in the corners of his feeble mind till I drove him mad, taking such pleasure in revealing him to be not even a mere peasant.

I swallowed hard, struggling against the knot of grief in my windpipe.

'He was the first, and the last. He was wrong.'

Kruhen Chay gaped at me in amusement, so stunned was he by my words. His reaction to what I had hoped was a war cry gave me a nauseous feeling in the pit of my stomach, as though he'd just shrunk me down to the carpet.

It must be entertaining to have such a lively imagination. I have slain every other useless Guardian who dared to face me, you pathetic child. What makes you think you, not even yet Guardian, will be any different?

'Because he was wrong,' I repeated.

It dawned on me then, slowly, magnificently.

He was wrong.

You cannot rid the world—or yourself—of darkness. You cannot fight it as you would any other enemy. It will always exist, and it will always confront you; that is the price we pay for being human. And that, I realized, was why not a single Guardian had ever survived. They threw themselves against the darkness like a drowning man upon the rocks; eventually, they broke.

But you cannot oppose the darkness by making yourself an obstacle to it. There was only one way, I saw, to combat the darkness—to go through it.

Kruhen Chay lunged at me, finally sick of my babbling, with a furious snarl. But I didn't turn away. Before he could change course, I took a deliberately large step forward. When I felt my front toes brush merrily against the carpet, I sucked in one last deep breath before jumping straight at the oncoming darkness, forcing myself to think of the fireplace beyond.

And then I was flying.

And then I was misery . . . I was the cries of lost children, sobbing for their home. I was the sound of bullets striking the sky, ripping it to pieces. I was the whistling of a hundred faded bits of blood-red string, sinking against the wall of an empty mosque. I was the bitter, stale air of Kashmir, longing for the wind. I was the desperate clanging of an empty well, a dull and hollow block of stone. I was the paradise lost.

And then I was nothing at all.

And then I was light.

The slam of my bones against frost-cold marble brought me back to the present. I felt my jaw shudder from the impact, waited as many seconds as I dared, and forced myself to stand. Kruhen Chay was writhing like a startled lizard, his back to me, hissing and scraping his nails against the centre of his deformed body. Without sparing either him or his then screeching accomplice another glance, I pressed my filthy hand to the crest. I was so weak and wobbly I could barely move. I hadn't expected it to be enough. But something from deep within the crest had caught my wrist like a magnet, and was pulling me closer every moment.

The crest locked around my palm, cracks in the brick surrounding cool marble closing up as it shimmered, and suddenly I could feel something moving beneath my fingers. It was smooth, delicate and utterly beautiful. Despite the knowledge in my heart that this fight was not nearly over, my muscles unwound and relaxed beneath my skin.

The warmth of the magic began to move past my fingers, over my wrist, a velvet glove.

With a sudden surge, I felt it gush through all of me at once, as though each of my cells was swelling and bursting and forming anew. I would have screamed, but it coated my vocal cords like syrup, shining out from within me so that I could feel rays of light gleaming out from my body.

I collapsed beside the fireplace. Yet I was no longer shivering. I simply lay there like a forgotten rag doll in the wreckage of a fire, with nowhere to go and nothing to go to and no way to get there if I did.

I rose to my feet.

Something light and powerful was surging through my heart.

My body seemed no longer to need encouragement or even instructions.

I was ready.

No, snarled Kruhen Chay, his voice no longer an omnipresent siren's call but the shattered, feeble whining of a bratty child.

You . . . you . . .

He turned savagely on Mr Bhukhari, as though noticing him for the first time. With a brutal slice, he cut through the darkened flesh on his victim's ear. It did not bleed red but oozed a thick, black sludge that dripped down the side of his face and joined Kruhen Chay once more, shattering their connection at last.

Mr Bhukhari took a single step back, as though trying to escape from his own body. He dropped to his knees, form contorted. A guttural wail tore from him as he shrunk before me, suffocating darkness flooding out of him. His hair began to recede and turned a foggy, miserable grey.

'Traitor!' he roared, sinking into himself as he clutched at his mutilated face. 'I did what you asked! I brought you the house!'

And you are no longer of use to me, finished Kruhen Chay, not even looking at his former ally. *I'm amazed you didn't foresee this. As if I'd waste my time helping your people form a nation once I had all I needed from you. Like a fool you let me use your body, helped me acquire a powerful form! Further proof of how impossibly incompetent and overconfident humans are. So much so, in fact, that while I took your body, you refused to allow me access to your mind. If you had, it might perhaps have saved your worthless life.*

He paused, as though unsure whether it was worth his time to continue. When he spoke again, his voice hummed with malicious pleasure.

Of course, your unwillingness didn't stop me.

'What?' gasped Mr Bhukhari, barely able to form words, eyes wide and watery from the smoke, his limbs going limp against him.

You think I'd allow a human to make my decisions for me? I have had control over your mind since the moment I entered you, fool. I played along with your little game; I kept you conscious, let you believe you were in charge. You were far less trouble that way. But they were my triumphs, every one of them, all of them weakening my ancient foe. Bombing the police station, armies pouring funds into shrapnel, using this force to keep control and firing to kill, regardless of whom the bullet struck, this violent bitterness against your nation that spreads like contagion . . . Did you ever, even for a second, truly believe that you *had the power to keep me out?*

In my mind's eye, I saw an inflamed, red eyeball, staring without seeing, contorted in pain, bits of metal sinking slowly into its flickering iris. I saw a hailstone of rocks showering from the sun. And I realized that we were far more tainted by the darkness than any of us anywhere knew, above all, the man writhing on the carpet before me.

Mr Bhukhari let out a bellow of pain, of fear, of emptiness, betrayed by the devil inside himself. For all but a second, his gaze caught mine, brimming with tortured sadness. And not even the most skilled cryptographer could have deciphered all that swirled within the sunken depths of his eyes. Then he collapsed against the ground, so near death that his body seemed to have begun its decay already, his sagging skin turning to festered flesh against his charred skull, and Kruhen Chay kicked him uncaringly aside.

The darkness willed me to drown in his burnt, rotting face, willed me to choke from the smoke surrounding his figure, nearly lured me within the reach of his subtly glinting claws.

But I would never do that again.

I had seen him for what he really was—a shadow.

And I was no longer afraid of the dark.

I stood firmly before the fireplace, blocking his escape route, and felt the magic thrumming in my bones, waiting eagerly for the charge. The flames glowed brighter behind me.

Suddenly, with a fleeting glance at me, he burst out of the living room, trailing putrid smoke, hell-bent on destroying all he could of the house—his hated enemy that yet battled against his rise to power and dominance. I knew what he was after, what he had always been after: the removal of his final obstacle. For then he would sink deep within the once fertile earth, poison every tree, let every flower rot, hack at every hilltop, mar every sunrise and fester within every decaying heart. He would fuse with Kashmir itself, the land and my people surrendering to him and his suffocating, cruel darkness, fire and blood ruling as his fellows. And he would be indestructible. Without hesitation, I chased after him, so quickly it seemed I was plummeting from all that I had been to all that I was then.

The banister bore the long scratches of his claws, and the bedroom door hung by a single, fractured hinge, bent over like a forgotten lover, a vine of hope preventing her from leaving a silent grave.

I came expecting cries of pain, yells of fury and the wreckage of loss. What I heard instead were whoops of encouragement and bangs of celebration.

Kruhen Chay had become tangled in squirming bed sheets, and the portraits were, of course, the ones making all the noise. As I watched, the Mughal warrior launched his gleaming, unused spear out of his frame and straight at Kruhen Chay. It soared through the air, a miracle of creation, and landed squarely on target, covering Kruhen Chay with a splatter of white and grey paint. His look of incredulity nearly made me smile; he had clearly not expected the *house* to put up such a fight.

'Excellent work!' came the tinkling voice of the empress. 'I could have shot it better myself, of course, but . . .'

'Dear,' the emperor was muttering, 'I'm the ruler, I think I'm supposed to give the orders . . .'

'Please just stop arguing, whatever else you do!' came the noise of the normally quiet mantri, who was in the process of scribbling so furiously on the scroll in front of him that he had ink on his glasses. 'I'm trying to copy down the court proceedings, and I'll muddle it up with you yelling like that.'

In a wave of untamed brutality, Kruhen Chay struck at the bed sheet with a jagged claw. The sound of ripping fabric propelled me forward, and, feeling every element within the house bind itself to me, I focused upon a single spot beneath me, launching a nail from the cracking floor into his eye. With a bellow, he released the ravaged bed sheet, who sunk, defeated, to the floor. As he clutched his face, I saw his edges grow light and blurred.

He went for the portraits next, his aim on the back wall, snarling at the Kashmiri seated furthest left; the one who had first trapped him in his steaming prison. His claws began to cut through the faded bronze frame like butter, sawing at wood shavings and twisted bits of metal, melting them as he went—and instantaneously they shuddered to a halt, just before they reached the painting itself. Spluttering, he turned to see me, my arms trembling with the strain of holding him back, the rush of power flooding through me directed straight at his struggling limbs.

Beginning to sweat (which I hardly ever do), but smiling still, I launched him out of the bedroom in one swift move. He tumbled like a misshapen cricket ball down the hallway and into the library.

The Pandit seemed completely unperturbed by these proceedings and sat nonchalantly in his damaged frame. Smoothing his single bunched up tuft of hair, where the paint had smudged slightly as it melted from the heat of the darkness, he took the opportunity to begin narrating the nature of consciousness to anyone who would listen.

After silently thanking my ancestors for their obsession with unnecessarily large and extravagant frames, I hurried towards the library.

My bare feet felt the scorching heat of the wood, and I looked down to see stains of faded black against the ground, dark footsteps of a clumsy thief.

I was so occupied with examining the wood that I slammed straight into the closing door.

I burst in with an exclamation of shock and pain, and the sight that greeted me only added to it. A tidal wave of yellow paper and hard book covers were soaring through the air, straight at the doorway. For a moment, I believed they were soaring towards me, and I was on the verge of stopping them with a rush of magic, when I realized they were aiming for Kruhen Chay, then a shrunken, faded figure, cowardly compared to his earlier grandeur. He let out a muffled, garbled yell as he was buried under a mountain of books.

It seemed that the armchair was directing the attack, and directing it very systematically at that. He was puffing out a long string of precise words, riding on one large gulp of air.

'27, 82, straight to his head, 90, 120, now, hit him with the pointed end first, 32, 68, cover up that stray limb . . .'

Abruptly, his chain of orders was snapped in half by the cries of his troops and the screech of tearing paper.

I moved forward and focused on paralysing Kruhen Chay. A ball of enchanted energy then encompassed the shuddering swarms of binding and paper, shining golden with light, yet rippling with darkness beneath, and I tried to think of how I would get him out of the library with half the library on top of him. It turned out I didn't need to worry.

It seemed that the bookshelves cared more for their books than they had ever let on.

With bangs that would put a chaotic firework display to shame, they knocked each other over, beginning from the very last bookshelf and continuing in one smooth wave to the very first. The thudding grew louder and louder, till they sounded like a pride of lions breaking into a chorus of roars. I threw my arms up over my head, hearing the fleet of bookshelves collide, crash and sink.

When they quieted, I raised my head to see that the final bookshelf had landed squarely upon Kruhen Chay, pinning him down to prevent his escape, and had halted just inches from the door. Long, brown scrapes against the ceiling gave the appearance of a wild beast having tried frantically to dig its way out.

At first, I had a sudden urge to push the bookshelves upright once more, lest their worn wood catch fire from the heat of Kruhen Chay. But it seemed he was no longer the blaze he had once been.

The books, however, had not been spared the bookshelves' attack.

'Would it kill you to lose a few pounds?'

'I think we all ought to take a nice, deep breath . . .'

'Everyone—all puzzles have an answer. Think your way out of this, come on.'

'Are you up for a quick debate on that?'

'If it's still raining, I'm not coming out!'

I laughed softly to myself, still concentrating all my energy on that single point on my fingertips from which I could feel heat emanating, fighting to keep my enemy immobile.

A memory from an old, unlabelled bottle surfaced before me; fishing on a still, gentle lake, leaning out of the side of the tilting shikara, watching as women wove near the water weeds, holding tight to the merry rod as something struggled fiercely beneath.

'Get off him!' I yelled at last. 'I can't hold him forever!'

With a single whoosh, the light within me erupted in a tidal wave that gushed through the library, and I had shoved the bookshelf above Kruhen Chay into a standing position once more. It stood, empty and alone, in the middle of the room. Slowly, steadily, eyes closed in concentration yet sensing the magic around me, I began to drag the splatter of darkness that remained out from under the jumble of books. I tried to steer him away from those who I could see were badly torn. I could feel each slice in their yellowed pages, as though it were a jagged knife grating against my own neck.

But his power was formidable yet, and he fought to regain control of his limbs. As he did so, I noticed that some were beginning to shrink; they seemed to be melting into thick crude oil. Perhaps those weren't footsteps I'd seen earlier.

I had allowed it to distract me a second too long. Kruhen Chay had broken my shaking amateur hold, and he slammed past me at once, snaking down the stairs. Clutching my shoulder, I pelted past him, skidding so badly it seemed that the floor was indeed slicked in oil.

I could hear the fire crackling, cutting off his first route of escape; and yet he had not made for the living room at all.

Panic echoed dimly around me.

Oh, no . . . oh, no . . . don't let him reach that door, Zoon . . . don't let him reach that door!

I stumbled on the last step and tumbled down into the front room, narrowly missing hitting my head against the wall. My heart thudded heavily for a moment, trying to prove to me that we were okay, I was still alive, I was working fine.

Kruhen Chay had sped towards the door, but the chair had no intention of letting him leave; with a war cry that sounded suspiciously like 'Die, devil, die!' he launched himself at the door handle and barricaded it from the inside.

Kruhen Chay let out a snarl of undiluted fury and flashed a deep black once more. He was quickly regaining whatever strength the house had managed to take from him, and he slashed uncontrollably at the quixotic quill, who had taken it upon himself to spear out his eye.

But it would hardly have mattered even if he'd grown another limb—I knew what to do.

'Now!' I cried out, and before I had even finished the word, cracks had begun forming against each plank of wood on the walls; they trembled with the strain. Time stood still, frozen in awe, and the pipes burst from the walls, like hidden dragons, with a shattering splintering of wood. Each pipe threw itself forward, eager to enter the battlefield, free from the dark at last.

Blasts of mist jetted across the room so that my eyes blurred and became useless; Kruhen Chay's cries rang horribly through the room, growing fainter and fainter.

I raised my hands in front of me and made to clear the air . . . and he emerged, thrashing and convulsing against the steam as it leached the misery from his surface, spitting out a long rush of furious, fuming words.

I watched, as though the hourglass had slowed, as Kruhen Chay was thrown against the ground. He was melting, all of him, the black tar of his limbs losing shape. He stuck to the ground like chewed gum, spitting out enraged insults that grew quieter and quieter, until his voice was a hoarse memory of yesterday.

Just then, I heard another unfamiliar noise—the thick, gentle sound of shifting cloth. The carpet, who, to my knowledge, had never so much as looked out of the window, was moving. Steadily, smilingly, she twisted herself over at her right corner, so that I caught a glimpse of a metal handle beneath her thick, elegant fabric.

The handle was bloated and rusty, so disfigured from years of disuse that it no longer resembled a handle at all. Yet when I touched it, it leapt open as though it had been waiting for me all its life.

It led down into some sort of cave. I leaned in closer and was met with a gust of steam. It tasted stale and lifeless. My stomach coiled around my ribs in fear and comprehension.

The hammam.

Over my shoulder, Kruhen Chay slumped weakly against the chair's steady legs, flopping about uselessly like a headless cockroach.

I closed my eyes for a moment and took a deep breath. Then I felt my magic release the panting quill on to the haggard desk. It was like a pinpoint of life within the vast darkness of my closed lids.

Slowly, steadily, I coaxed it to curl around Kruhen Chay, sealing the steam around him. Then, after pulling the bonds tight to form a rope, I pulled Kruhen Chay closer and closer.

Just before he reached me, I opened my eyes. Still he tried to fight against the invisible cords around him. In a single movement, I flung the bundle of darkness down into the hammam.

As he neared the cave where he'd once been entrapped for hundreds of long, grinding years, its hidden entrance began to slowly bend open with a horrible creak, as though it, too, had been waiting. The screech of metal and stone boomed in the normally silent hammam. Layers of dust began to flow like water from the sudden unprecedented disturbance.

And below that, it was too dark for the sun's rays, cowardly despite their bright bravado, to pierce. It was the dark of creatures that are slow and old, lingering on the edge of life, yet unclaimed by an uncaring death.

Something rose then, from the very corner of the hammam—a figure, unmoving, white and deathly pale, as though ill. His eyes seemed white and pupil-less, and I could see the worn wood of the ground right through him. He rose, moving towards me, passing straight through rusty heaters . . . and yet, somehow, I felt no urge to dodge a possible attack. I knew him somehow . . . he was my friend.

He flew past me, slowly, gently, as though he had not seen the world for a hundred years and was almost frightened of what he might find. He inclined his head towards me. He very nearly smiled. Then he drifted up to the fireplace and rose up through the chimney. I could no longer see him at all. There wasn't a shred of evidence that he'd even existed.

The roar of my enemy, still putting up a stubborn fight, brought me harshly back to earth. He fought against my hold; I gritted my teeth with the effort to keep steady.

He gasped in pain; his struggles subsided as the steam held him fast in its iron hold. Scriptures engraved aeons ago in the stone began to glow and twist, melting and freezing anew.

As I forced him to enter his miserable cavern, he let out a final, raspy cry of bitterness and anger and unquestionable loss. He turned once more to stare at me, his newly translucent, emaciated body twisting horribly as he did so, the cracks meant to serve as his mouth twisting in hatred . . .

There was a crash as stone thudded against the ground, sealed once more.

He was gone.

Gone for now, I told myself, calming my heaving lungs. I gave a great sigh and continued to breathe deeply till the air entering my body felt nearly the same as the air leaving it.

Then I stood up.

All at once, the walls detonated into deafening cheers. I allowed a smile to slide across my lips.

As I walked into the living room, they continued to hoot and clap.

'What a show! I really enjoyed the light effects!' called the quill eagerly.

'Ugh, ignore him! You were fantastic! What a feat, what a battle to have fought, especially at your age! I never expected it. I'll say quite frankly . . .' the fireplace put in.

'Completely brilliant!' roared the king's portrait. 'I'm proud to have you serving in my court!'

'I agree, sahib! That was, hands down, the most memorable court proceeding ever!'

'Yes, I must say,' put in the watercolour Pandit, 'it seems I was quite a fitting source of guidance and inspiration.'

'Very well done,' came the steady, calming tone of the armchair from the library. 'I was leaning towards taking a different route, but your way was better, I must say.'

'Armchair,' I murmured in a tentative, hushed voice, suddenly unsure of my post as Guardian, 'do you think I made the right choice? About not trying to destroy Kruhen Chay, I mean.'

He didn't say anything for a moment. When he did, I could hear a smile in his voice. It wasn't joyous; it was a sad, gentle, quiet sort of smile.

'Yes,' he replied softly. 'Such a thing would be impossible, Zoon. Darkness is now as much a part of every human as light is; there will always be darkness somewhere in the world and in us. What is important is that we do not let it control us.'

I nodded. For some reason, I thought of Tathi.

'But it is clear that you understand that already,' said the armchair, in a lighter, encouraging tone. 'The resilience and resistance this house displayed today showed powerful magic; it has proved that your spirit is braver and stronger than any other Guardian we have ever had.'

My smile grew wider, and I felt a rush of pride in my chest.

The books continued slapping their pages together and cheering deafeningly, oblivious to this quiet exchange, rowdy and rough as a full cricket stadium.

And then, so silent that I could almost believe it had been wishful thinking, I heard the softest and gentlest of voices coming from beneath me.

'That was really something, wasn't it? For a minute there, I was really scared that you'd hurt yourself.'

I knelt down and patted the carpet gently. 'You made sure I didn't,' I replied. 'Thank you!'

'And thank you to all of you,' I called out, beginning to feel like I'd just won some kind of award. 'You helped me so much . . . and . . . hold up . . .' The tiniest of gears inside me stuttered to a stop, clogged by an interesting observation. 'Wait a minute . . . how can all of us hear each other if we're in separate rooms?'

There was a moment of dead silence, like when a bride spills rogan josh on her best sari an hour before the wedding. Then the house exploded all over again, only this time in a chorus of laughter.

'What, did you think you'd become Guardian and everything would stay the same?' called the fireplace.

'She thought she'd fight Kruhen Chay and then just go about her business as usual!' joked the armchair, and the desk practically broke a leg sniggering. I couldn't help but grin.

I turned round to face the house. 'Guys,' I said loudly, in what I hoped was an authoritative enough voice for them not to start laughing again, 'Ma's going to be home soon with Tathi and we need this place cleaned up. I know we can't fix everything, but let's try to do what we can. Okay?'

To my utter amazement, they all began following my instructions right away. A little ray of pride, like the candle on a birthday cake, sparked inside me.

I decided to do this systematically, room by room. While the fireplace worked on sucking in all the smoke he'd dispensed and shoving it up the chimney, I straightened out the desk, mended the quill's torn feather slowly (he just wouldn't stop going on and on about it—his 'battle scar' he called it), the magic gentler then, and, with just a touch, I was able to restore the shine to the desk's tattered surface.

The floorboards took a while to mend, what with their splintered edges and nails jutting out, but I managed it. I left the walls as they were; I couldn't make sense of the maze of pipes tangled with shattered wood.

Once the carpet had been cleaned out (which took surprisingly little time), I moved upstairs.

Halfway up, I caught a glimpse of the quiet garden outside. A bright blush of chocolate brown was creeping rapidly up the chinar, sealing jagged cracks, filling the air with a sugary scent and growing small spots of green as it meandered. I gave the banister an excited little squeeze.

The bedroom was really quite a mess. It didn't take me long to mend the brave bed sheet, though, magic dancing from my fingertips; she was then promptly greeted with a round of fierce applause as she slept tiredly, yet happily, on the bed once more. But I'd no idea what to do with the Pandit's desecrated frame.

Finally, I settled on mending the metal links within it as best I could. Hopefully, it would be enough to avoid awkward questions.

As I healed the house, restoring whatever I could to its former majesty, I felt it resonate within me, a talisman of sunshine.

In the desperate hope that some of it at least might have righted itself by the time I got there, I checked on the library last. I should have known better than to do that. The books seemed to have become far more confused than usual, fighting over torn pages, toppling over one another and jostling for space in the only standing bookshelf, who was then dangerously close to falling over once again.

I buried my face in my hands before even beginning.

Deciding that this would be a lot easier if I could just see past the flurry of pages, I moved all the books to one small corner with a sweep of my arm. This rush of magic only fuelled their zest and chatter further, although those with missing pages paused and stuttered, lost for words.

After a great deal of effort, which involved having to suspend certain bookshelves in the air while reorganizing their neighbours, I'd managed to get the bookshelves back into respectable order.

'Not bad,' I muttered to myself. Sure, a few of them were crooked, and yes, they did have plenty of bumps and scratches, and, of course, some of them may have been upside down, but it wasn't too shabby for a first try.

The books were, if anything, even more frustrating. Eventually I was forced to immobilize them while I read through every single torn page to determine which book it belonged to. Once they found themselves whole again, they began to fly back to their places on the shelves.

With the library then looking as though it had been hit by a natural disaster of slightly lesser intensity, I trooped downstairs once more.

'Zoon! What do I do with this old thing?' called the fireplace as he chucked glowing embers at a small pile of ashes on the ground beside him.

'What is that?'

I leaned closer to get a clear look—it wasn't all ashes. Some of it looked like dead skin . . .

'That's Mr Bhukhari.'

With a lurch that nearly made me sick, I launched myself backwards.

'Ew! Gross! Why is he—it—on the carpet? Get it out!'

'Where do you propose I put it?'

'Just chuck it out of the chimney!'

The fireplace inhaled sharply, partly because I'd told him to and partly because my hysterics irritated him. The small lump of black rot, then all that was left of what had once been an unbroken, strong, healthy man, whooshed up the chimney as he did so. With a single large gust of air, he proclaimed it far away already.

'Why did that happen to him?' I whispered, still horrified by what I'd just seen.

'When you give all inside you to darkness,' the fireplace replied, 'it leaves you nothing but an empty shell. He left his life in the hands of a creature known to deceive and betray.'

We were silent for a moment. I hadn't thought I cared for that man. But I did. How horrific it had been to watch him descend further into the darkness and his maze of thorns, into manipulation and madness, into his own shrivelled heart. I imagined him as a younger man, seated at dinner with his family, happy and hopeful and whole. Somehow, death is always painful, no different for your greatest enemy than for your closest companion—and he was somewhere inexplicably in between. It leaves a bitter taste in the air; a taste of sickness, sudden fear and lost opportunity.

Just then, I heard the grating twist of a key in our lock.

'Ma's home.'

Chapter Ten

Something was wrong the moment she entered. The air came in, and it was too chilly. Too brutal.

Her shoes were soaked with something thick and dark.

Her dupatta, her best dupatta, was torn. Right down the middle. Dimly, I registered that it had been torn there before, and the house had mended it. Or rather, hadn't mended it well enough.

And then my eyes travelled up to her face.

Her eyes were brimming with salty waves, as sincere as a sailor's song begging the winds to guide his ship back home.

I sat down suddenly, veins flooded with blood. I did not need to hear her say it. I did not want to hear her say it. For her to confirm what I already knew would make it somehow inescapable.

The chair, I then noticed, was still overturned. There were splinters sticking out of the ground. The walls I couldn't fix were yet burst open, pipes hanging out at odd angles, steam still smoking forth from some of them. A fine layer of dust settled about us. In the other room, the last embers of the fire spluttered loudly and went out. And yet neither of us spoke.

Every part of me was a piece of scrap metal left out in the rain; I had rusted, and was scraping at the slightest movement. A large brick with sharp, grated edges had been dropped inside my aching head and was proceeding to throw itself about with as much force as it could muster.

For once, the house was quiet.

I wished they would speak. I did not want their sadness, their sympathy, their silence. I was desperate to distract myself in any way I could.

'Zoon,' she began.

'No,' I whispered. 'Ma, please, please, don't, don't say it, don't . . .' I continued, louder then.

She took in a great breath of air.

'How?' I asked, begging as the hawkers beg for sales, begging as the people beg for peace, begging as Kashmir has always begged, has always been forced to.

'Heart attack.'

Her voice was choked; the words were a crushing row of chilled, dead fingers in her windpipe.

'Because of the bomb.'

She was wrong. It was something I simply knew, as though someone had carved it against the inside of my skull. But it was no longer a startling revelation so much as a dull ache for a happier time, a happier place, a happier way to die.

Slayed every other useless Guardian . . . His words began like a forest fire in the quiet meadows of my mind, destroying everything in their path. I buried my eyes in my hands to fight the pain.

But I was tied to Tathi's death as I had been to her life, and my grief collected in my bones like steaming pools of acid.

Ma moved to lean her umbrella against the wall.

I froze. I could not tear my gaze away from that umbrella, from that mouldy, ripped, old, brown umbrella, that bent, broken, useless umbrella that she'd just put in its proper place.

And it was then that I knew we'd go on. We'd go on, shattered, perhaps, miserable, of course, broken, without a doubt . . . but we'd go on.

Because in all that had happened in just one day, in all that we'd been through, in all that we'd lost, and in all the misery we were yet to face, it was still important that the umbrella was put back against the wall.

The radio lying wearily in the corner, clearly worse off for the battle it had witnessed, abruptly crackled to life. Ma walked over and began twiddling with the lifeless dials, trying to switch to the news channel. I gazed dazedly out of the window. The dusty brown streets were deserted. An old newspaper bearing near-black tyre tracks was sunken into the centre of the road, unfluttering. Curtains were drawn, doors were shut, curfew was obeyed. My home, I realized, was very much like the moon: bright and mesmerizing, a favourite of painters, yet covered with craters on every inch of land.

'Currently no news on the arrest and capture—'

'Zoon!' Ma implored. 'Listen, this might be important!'

I didn't want to listen. I knew it wasn't important, any of it. We'd all heard it as many times as we'd taken a breath of life. But any distraction from my mind was welcome.

'The bomb was triggered at exactly forty minutes past seven in the evening by a band of militants calling for aazadi.'

I felt sick to my stomach.

Freedom.

Was that what Tathi had got?

I tried to tune it out. I didn't know why it should suddenly make me nauseous; it was my childhood lullaby, this constant refrain of these bloodstained houses that I'd learnt to recognize as a war cry.

For some reason, my ears seemed bent on staying sharp and alert, picking up the whoosh of every gust of wind, fighting to find a way out.

'As of now it is unclear as to whether or not they were acting on behalf of a larger extremist organization. Indian troops moved in to restore order and have, we can confirm, fired directly at the militants responsible for the violence. However, this only seemed to have worsened conditions as riots continued and the legality of weapons used against the protesters and indirectly the wounded has come into question.'

Did the radio know what it was blaring out? Or did it just speak as commanded, on and on, day after day, with no understanding of what its words actually meant?

'The chaos has now begun to recede, although authorities are offering no comment on the identities of the perpetrators. The Indian prime minister has, in the last half an hour, delivered a statement declaring imminent negotiations.'

'Ma, can we shut it off?' I burst out. She nodded, staring at the carpet. I doubted she'd even heard.

'This just in, the chief minister soon to visit—'

A sharp click pierced the cool air, and the voice was cut off immediately.

For a few moments, no one said anything. The light around me came on too quick, in fragmented flashes that I couldn't prepare myself for.

'Zoon,' Ma said, and I didn't need to look up; I could hear her tears in her cracking voice.

'Let's say a prayer. For Tathi. All right?'

I nodded, feeling my cheeks grow chilly and wet.

I took in a great, sickly sniff before beginning.

And we sang. Softly, perhaps, but the song rang through the walls, and the cracks in the walls, and I hoped that somehow, no matter where they were, the people of Kashmir could hear it.

When we were finished, Ma rose to move towards the cooking range. 'I'd been saving this for tomorrow,' she muttered.

From one of our oldest, creakiest cupboards, she took out a rough earthen pot. All along the side, carved women danced together in one unbroken line, the occasional face disfigured by a drop of water. After removing the lid, she offered it to me.

The sweet scent of boiling rice and sugared milk wafted up around me, and my aching head seemed to grow light with the aroma. Despite how heavy and useless I felt, sitting there like a rock, the corners of my mouth began to twitch upwards.

'You made kheer!'

Ma wiped her eyes on the back of her torn dupatta, but not before I'd caught a glimpse of her quietly growing smile.

'Happy birthday, Zoons.'

We sat together on the bottom step, gradually emptying the chilled pot, content to take comfort in the mundane, even if for just a moment. The kheer felt frosty against my tongue, the crunch of almonds like the hatching of an egg inside my mouth. It was a most welcome feeling . . . An uncomfortable warmth yet lingered in the air.

Finally, when we were beginning to scrape the glinting white off the bottom of the bowl, what with the weight of the dessert in our stomachs and the veil of prayer against our grief, I felt that it was the time to ask her what I'd been meaning to ask since the moment she entered the door.

'Ma,' I began, 'I know that this may not be the best moment for you, but I really need to ask—will you still insist that our house be sold?'

I expected a flow of well-practised, ready answers to tumble down immediately from her sure lips.

But she was quiet. Thinking? Considering? I hoped so.

After what seemed to me like the reign of an entire dynasty, she replied.

'Well . . . I've really no idea where Mr Qureishi has gone. Or even Mr Bhukhari, come to think of it. Or—' She gestured wildly around her. 'What on *earth* happened here? He was in the living room, wasn't he?'

I opened my mouth, begging my muddled brain to come up with some sort of a reply.

'Oh, but you wouldn't know,' Ma cut in. 'You were in your room with the door shut . . . weren't you?'

'Yeah, yeah of course I was.'

'Good. I'm glad you stayed safe. It wasn't smart of me to leave you home with a stranger as it is,' she sighed.

'So . . .' I continued, trying to put the pieces together to form a clear image, 'if you don't know where they are, especially now since we need all this repaired, it'll be much harder to sell. Right?'

She nodded bleakly. 'And now I'm sure the number of buyers will have collapsed, given what's just happened,' she added.

'But it's okay,' I put in, trying to comfort her while simultaneously hiding my selfish glee. 'I mean, we just heard it on the radio. The violence won't be that bad any more.'

She gave a light laugh.

'These things happen all the time, Zoon. How are you suddenly so sure that this time will be different?'

Her words reminded me of something else. Something now locked so deep within the earth that his cries would turn to stone before they reached the surface.

'Oh, I've just got a good feeling about it.'

'Right. Sure.'

She pulled me into a tight hug. I buried myself within her, almost wanting to be a baby again, locked safely within someone else, separated from the torture of emotion by a thick layer of flesh.

I inhaled deeply. She smelled of lavender, of fresh grass, of rows of apple trees against the mountains, of home. Whatever home meant any more.

'Besides,' I heard her whisper, so softly that I wondered whether I was even meant to hear it, 'it's not what Tathi would have wanted.'

In the days that followed, life was no longer distinguishable from a dream. Everything was a gentle haze, like a shikara ride from one bank to the next, when the lake is still and the waters a navy blue. Thoughts were short and singular, never scratching beneath the surface, for those that did, inevitably led to pain.

I cleaned often. It didn't take me much—an hour, a daydream, a little bit of magic—but it was a great comfort to Ma. A clean house to her meant a fresh start, a tranquil heart, a tidy mind.

The street was quiet and still, waiting patiently for tomorrow, when they hoped the weather would improve. A few boys tossed an apple back and forth down the road. Their chappals slapped against the mud, upsetting little puffs of dirt and sweeping them away.

People came to mend the roads, the houses, the hearts. Life began to flow again, just as it always had. But haltingly, carefully, cautious then of pain.

We received scattered flowers, kind words and the occasional hug of greeting.

We seemed to give them away as quickly as they came.

Noise was unbearable, and silence even more so.

The funeral was held in a small, overgrown clearing near Shankaracharya temple. Over the tops of the thinning trees, its gold-and-red flag flapped wildly in the wind, reminding us that had we been more fortunate, we could have been standing under its silver roof rather than beholding it.

She deserved more. She always had. But I didn't know what else to give her; and if I did, I didn't know how else to do it.

Before the others began to arrive, I'd walked round and round the same track in the clearing as though it had been marked out for me, pointing my fingertip at the occasional weed or tall stem of grass, shrinking it down to something respectable.

The prasad and other snacks had been laid out against a pure white tablecloth, courtesy of Rani Auntie, who was, for the first time, painfully purged of yellow. Picnic mats and bed sheets had been spread out across the field.

A small wood-fire, lit in some sort of iron pan, was at the centre of it all. We could not cremate her body because we were not yet allowed access near the bomb site; currently, the area was flooded with quick-tempered policemen and still brimming with unspoken unrest. It had not been openly declared, of course, but what with one thing and another, we'd decided it was better to be safe than shot.

People began to trickle in, slowly at first, then steadily, confidently, like a leaky tap, till, finally, every mat was filled. Voices came hushed and delicate, like nightingales in the woods. It was all a blur—names, faces, tears.

I could smell incense from the black sticks shoved roughly into large potatoes. They stood like ancient rocks over the grass. It twisted horribly in my nose, and I coughed, brushing it away. The smoke had brought back memories that I was not yet ready to face.

A man I had never seen before was reading out prayers from a thick sheaf of pages clamped in his right hand, cramming her name in here and there so people wouldn't forget who it was they mourned.

The pages seemed almost charred with age. I wondered if the book was made simply to avoid too much hassle at such events—a compact, time-efficient farewell.

The sky had become a tender blue. It seemed like the deepest ocean, expanding ahead of us, with enchanting and bizarre creatures lurking beneath its murky surface, waiting to be discovered. I did not know whether it would last.

Kehva was passed around in small, plastic cups that did nothing to keep the heat from biting into my palm. The almonds inside had grown soggy and limp; they slid down my throat like wriggling, squishy bugs.

I saw my mother, forbidden tears dripping down her flushed cheeks, and I realized that her hair swept in an undisturbed sheet around her shoulders, waving lazily at me from across the clearing. Her three friends stuck to her side like persistent vendors, offering free words of comfort with every hug accepted.

I walked closer, dropping to the grass and leaning against her knees. I felt her palm run through my frizzy hair.

Every sip of kehva seemed to light a flame within me, the blaze eating away at the pulsating sickness I felt inside my chest.

Chandani Auntie spoke in her usual exuberant tone, though slightly dulled to suit the occasion, like a bedside lamp at bedtime. I heard, but I did not listen. I did not think that she would ever say anything that could make me listen then.

It was nearly offensive, how wrong I was.

'I know how it is, Shanti. I know you feel as if they're not with you any more. But she is. Just as my son is with me.'

I turned so sharply my neck cricked painfully. She caught sight of my shocked, confused stare and leaned down so I could hear her better.

'My son, Arshad. He's gone now.'

'Gone?' I croaked. I seemed to have lost my voice. I wondered where it could have wandered off. Perhaps it had been washed away with the tears.

'Gone,' she repeated softly. 'They took him about two years ago. I suppose they must have seen him in too many protests to pretend he was just one of the crowd.'

I'd no idea how to respond. At another time, I might have given my condolences. But then, in the thick of mist and sadness, all inside me silent without searching for thought, I simply sat there and gazed at a patch of brown grass, turning this news over and over in my mind, as a gold miner examines a patch of shining dirt.

Chandani Auntie—the boisterous, loud-voiced Chandani Auntie, who always had a laugh in her throat, a smile on her lips and lipstick on her teeth—*our* Chandani Auntie, had seen pain greater than anything I'd ever dreamt her capable of withstanding.

'How?' I rasped again. 'How do you manage it?'

'Manage what, dear?' she murmured absent-mindedly.

'How are you so . . . so . . .'

'So happy?' she suggested, smiling gently at me.

I nodded vigorously.

'Sometimes I'm not,' she replied. 'Sometimes I feel as though I've sobbed away everything inside me, and there's nothing left to make me go on. I go to bed thinking I'll never find it in myself to wake up in the morning and carve. But you'll soon see, as I have, that time has an uncanny habit of passing when you least expect it to.'

I stared, rapt with attention, into her glowing brown eyes. Dimly I registered how strange it was to think you had known someone all your life, and then wake up one day to find you'd never known them at all.

'On those days when happiness does not come to me,' she continued, 'I discover happiness in what I can.'

I nodded slowly.

'I find it in the fields. I find it in my friends. And I find it in my son.'

I had forgotten to blink, and my eyes were beginning to water. But I refused to close them, even for a moment.

'Do you understand, Zoon?'

She wiped away the wet on my cheek.

'Yes,' I whispered. 'I think so.'

After yanking me up and into a crushing hug (she was still Chandani Auntie, after all), she rose once more with her hands clasped in front of her, eyes on the roaring fire.

The flames had begun to flicker madly, rippling the darkening air around us. Through the distorted evening, I saw a familiar sunny face, familiar except for the lack of a smile.

For the first time, my muscles wished to move of their own accord.

'Hi,' Altaf whispered when he saw me, and all at once, at the sight of him, a sharp image flashed before my mind: a chinar leaf, orange as the sinking sun, hidden in the shadow of its tree.

'Hi,' I responded, feeling my face grow hot. Suddenly, I wanted to be anywhere but there, standing directly in front of him, tears streaking my face, made instantly vulnerable by my grief.

Out of the corner of my eye, I saw Lameeya Auntie rush over to my mother, arms spread so wide she nearly knocked over the snacks table.

He handed me a crumpled piece of paper. I unwrapped it slowly to see a detailed sketch of my home, each brick shaded perfectly at the edges, each window glinting in the light, each leaf on the chinar rustling in the wind. A little girl and her mother waved cheerily up at me, an impossible peace surrounding them. My mouth fell open and a sharp sting pierced at my wet eyes.

'Listen,' Altaf muttered, breaking the stiff silence, 'I wanted to say that . . . I'm really sorry about what happened. And I'm . . . here to help if you need me.' I did not realize that he had taken my frigid hand until I looked down to see my fingers interlaced with his.

It didn't help my waterworks situation.

We sat down upon one of the mats spread out on the glistening grass, so old then that it was nothing more than a few tangled threads. My eyes stuck to the iron pan, above which the logs were crackling furiously. Beneath the rusty grills, there lay a sea of black, darker than midnight, softer than coal, as motionless as a memory. And fiery embers rained upon them, a constant shower of burning rocks, tinkling with the metal. They were beautiful, a golden dragon in the night sky, twisting against silver stars. And yet they lasted for less than a heartbeat, before melting away into their neighbours, vanishing into dust. Or, perhaps, I thought, turning to look at Altaf, his eyes bright even when there was nothing to see, they hid like buried treasure just beneath the surface, waiting to be discovered by someone who looked beyond the black.

A surge of light gushed into my slowly beating heart, not dissipating the sadness, but coating it with a sudden beam of strength, so that I felt unbreakable despite my misery and unshakeable in my actions. My veins thrummed within me, a blend of life and magic pressing against my skin.

I had loved Tathi more than even I would ever know. I loved her still, and I always would.

But I was also a Guardian.

Kashmir needed me.

I turned to Altaf, feeling every part of me beginning to come alive once more.

'You know once this is over, I'm going to keep taking you up on your promise of help.'

He grinned widely. It was oddly refreshing to see a happy face, like a chilled cup of juice in the unyielding summer heat.

'Of course. I'm part of the team, aren't I?'

The night came slow and shimmering, the stars blinking down at me through the window like a string of far-off fairy lights. The houses lay quiet, cosy in their closeness, the bundles of straw thrown up on their roofs making them appear like a flock of sheep trekking up to Shankaracharya Hill. The trees of the valley frolicked in the breeze, dancing in the haze of twilight, their bare branches no less graceful for the lack of a partner.

Inside, I could hear the gentle chatter of the fireplace downstairs, growing quieter as Ma put out his flames for the night. My limbs rested against the windowsill like uncoiled springs, supporting my lolling head. I let out a great sigh and heard her footsteps on the stairs.

I crawled into the blankets and tucked my knees under my chin, staring at the sketch on the windowsill, Altaf's name scrawled at the bottom. Beside me, Ma had climbed in as well, and was reading one of her favourite poems. She was squinting as she always did. I heard her mutter something under her breath about getting the Pandit a new frame. Smiling, I closed my heavy eyes. The mumbles from the portraits began to dim. The mattress had never felt so soft and deep, the bed sheet so like velvet, nor the bedroom, despite all my treasured memories, so much like home.

Epilogue

One Month Later

The garden has begun to blush green once more. The chinar's first magenta blossoms have begun to appear, dotting its firm, smooth wood. The clouds waft leisurely through the blue-green sky. The blanket of snow, a thick cocoon, has finally melted, allowing the butterfly of spring to burst forth in full bloom. The landscape is suffused with delicate brushstrokes: pinks, purples and a sheen of emerald. My heart grows lighter every day at the vibrancy of the paint. The *badamwari* have begun to blossom, stretching their branches out towards the sea of sunlight pouring in from the heavens.

The neighbours spread out their fraying chequered tablecloths, fresh hot meals on them. The head of the family leans against the bark of a tree. Their bubbling words are interspersed by the crunch of chana; my hand often grows tired from waving.

I had told myself that as the Guardian, wherever I saw signs of growing misery, I must hasten to alleviate it. But it seems my once chronic patient has no need of my treatment. Whatever splotches of darkness still manage to enter our lives can be overpowered by our laughter, our friendship and extraordinarily ordinary kindnesses.

For now, we have peace. New elections are to be held within a week. Danish Parvez, a young politician, has become the face of the leading party, taking the place of the old favourite, Mustafa Bhukhari. His words are cool raindrops against the smouldering hearts of the people, and they listen to him. Even so, hulking, sulking army men have been crammed into every crevice the government could find, and Rani Auntie does complain that they're ruining the pleasant weather.

Ma brought home a new clay pot yesterday with all the extra money she's been getting for her shawls. They're selling much faster now that the buses are coming to the valley again; visitors always seem far keener on her patterns than we are.

We've been keeping the pot on the desk beside the window so everyone can see him when they pass by. We're going to paint him together this afternoon. I'm thinking a turquoise-and-white blend, to remind me of the ocean, the deep shock of blue leading to a foam of white at the crests of its chattering waves. I've never seen it, but I hope to soon . . . it looks so lovely in the postcards. We're all most looking forward to hearing his first words. Despite the fact that we've no idea what he's like yet, the quill seems to already have found a best friend.

We'll be using whatever's left over to buy me the textbooks I've been wanting.

Tonight, Lameeya Auntie's bringing Altaf and his older brother over for dinner. Ma's eager to show off the newly mended walls; Bhasharat Uncle helped us out with them. Turns out he's quite handy with a toolbox. I do make it a point to stay out of her sight when she's cooking, though; she tends to be a bit antsy when the recipes get confusing.

Altaf and I have finished repairing the bukharis in the hammam. He asked, of course, numerous questions. I hadn't planned on answering so many; and yet he deserved the truth. We kept very quiet and worked quickly, that too only when Ma was out, but it wasn't nearly as difficult as I'd expected, thanks to my magic. Neither was it, to be honest, as dangerous as I had imagined it would be. I wonder if I'd weakened the darkness more than I thought. We still nailed the trapdoor shut, just in case.

Out in the garden, the red and gold of the flowers blend and fuse with one another against the sapphire sky, a school of fish darting through the shallow sea pools of the beach.

I lie down on the softly swaying grass and close my eyes. I don't mean to fall asleep, but the sunlight is warm against my face, the wind a perfect blanket, and somehow, I find myself beginning to dream.

And when I dream, the whole of Kashmir dreams with me.

Acknowledgements

I would like to thank my family—above all, my parents—for their help, guidance and inspiration. This book would not have existed without their love and support. I need to thank my friends as well, for telling me plainly and honestly if my ideas were rubbish. In particular, I would like to thank Shreya Raheja for boring me with a long-winded narrative about an extraordinary house in London, which blossomed into the beginnings of a novel.

I thank my school, Dhirubhai Ambani International School, and all my teachers for their continuous encouragement and understanding.

Endless thanks to Masood Hussain for his inspiration, time and sincere love for my work. You have helped shape *The House That Spoke* in ways I could never have imagined.

Sincere thanks to Rahul Pandita for inspiring me with his own work, bettering mine and for being a part of my journey.

I'm immensely grateful to Suhel Seth for bringing in new dimensions of creativity to this book.

I thank Penguin Random House India—especially Hemali Sodhi for having faith in my book before I did; Nimmy Chacko and Purnima Mahesh for striving to deliver above and beyond any expectations I had, and for playing such an important role in bringing *The House That Spoke* to life.

Many thanks to Fawkes for his friendship and wise counsel.

I thank Priyanka Ghose, Manoj Shroff and Ram Madhvani for their unbelievable patience and dedication, and for giving visuals to my dream.

And finally, thanks to my dogs, Toffee, Sugar, Fudge, Coco, Cherry and Fig, for being just the fluffy stress busters I needed at the end of a long day.